THE WIFE'S BABY

DANIEL HURST

www.danielhurstbooks.com

Download My Free Book

If you would like to receive a FREE copy of my psychological thriller 'Just One Second', then you can find the link to the book at my website www.danielhurstbooks.com

PROLOGUE

The door is locked and no matter how much I bang on it or shout for help, I know it's not going to be opened again.

Everyone was right. I should have just left it. I should have just got on with my life, or what was left of my life. But I ignored their advice.

I kept searching for the truth.

I refused to rest until I had answers.

Now I fear I'll never make it out of here alive.

I'm in the Scottish city of Stirling, or rather, I'm beneath it, locked away in this room that I should never have entered. It might seem like I'm in the wrong place at the wrong time, but the fact that I'm trapped tells me I am actually exactly where I need to be.

This is where I will find answers.

This is most likely where my daughter is.

I came to this city with my husband and our baby for a short holiday. In my mind, it was the perfect place for the three of us to come for a break. It was a trip that didn't involve having to go to an airport and enduring all the stress that such a place entails, nor did it require a particularly long train journey because we live just north of Edinburgh, meaning we could get here via public transport within an hour.

Visiting this historic city felt like a good idea at the time. It seemed like the perfect place for my husband and I to try and reconcile some of our irreconcilable differences. But perhaps I should have known better.

After all, the city is surrounded by a sweeping green landscape upon which many battles between the English and Scottish were fought. It only makes sense that it would also be the scene of another battle, a more modern one, between a warring wife and husband.

But this story isn't about me or the man I married - it's about our baby daughter.

I know she's here somewhere.

I also know the person who took her is on the other side of this door.

All I need to figure out now is how I can get out of here to get my revenge.

BEFORE

1

Deciding to have a holiday in Scotland in the middle of winter comes with risks. The cold is a given, but what if it's raining as well, and what if the rain is torrentially, relentlessly and devastatingly dreary? Weather like that would be enough to ruin any vacation. Fortunately, as I look out of the train window and catch a glimpse of Stirling Castle getting nearer in the distance, the rain clouds have left this part of the map alone. It's freezing out there, but the sky is a lovely blue, and it's one of those crisp winter days where outdoor surfaces are frosty, but the air is clean and fresh, and a person starts to think that this time of year might not actually be as bad as they thought it might be.

However, while we might have struck lucky with the weather for the start of our trip, there was still another risk to be taken into account regarding this holiday, and it's one that has nothing to do with the seasons and everything to do with the person sitting across the table from me on this train.

Leon, my partner of seven years and husband of four, has his head back on his seat and his eyes closed, meaning he's totally missing the pleasant view of the city that this train is gradually approaching. But I'm not going to give him a nudge and tell him to open his eyes for a couple of reasons. One, he's been to Stirling before, as have I, so as beautiful a place as it is, he has already seen it. Two, he was out late last night drinking with work friends, so I know he's hungover, despite him spending all morning trying to pretend to me that he isn't.

I can read him like an open book, and that's how I know he is feeling more than a little worse for wear. He's quieter when he's tired, more irritable when he's got a headache, and grouchier while carrying out typical everyday tasks. But the same could be said about most people, I suppose, so what's the one unique thing that my husband does that tells me, more so than anything else, that he is struggling with his overindulgence at the bar yesterday?

It's the fact he has an empty bottle of water on the table in front of him.

Leon hates water. He always says that it's boring and tasteless, and that's why he'll only ever consume it if it's mixed with something else like tea or orange squash. Most of the time, he survives on coffee, making an occasional exception for his favourite drink of all, lager. But today, he is guzzling water like there is a shortage of it coming, and that's how I know he is severely dehydrated and, therefore, very hungover.

Fortunately, I have no such issue myself, but that's because I'm sensible and act like a grown-up adult with grown-up responsibilities. I knew we had to be up early today to pack our things for this trip and catch our train, and that's why I made sure I was in bed at a sensible hour last night, unlike hubby, who staggered in after midnight and slept in the spare bedroom.

That's a place he has come to know very well recently.

But packing for this trip and making sure we were on time for this fifty-minute train journey from Edinburgh are not my only responsibilities. My biggest one is currently sitting on my lap, and as I look down at the beautiful baby girl with the bright blue eyes, I feel a mixture of pride and sorrow.

Pride because she is our girl, the fruits of mine and Leon's love.

And sorrow because that is a love that feels like it's extinguishing rapidly.

'No, Tuppence, that's not for you,' I say as I reach out and stop my daughter putting her father's water bottle lid in her mouth. At six months old, she's discovering the world more and more every day, and part of that discovery involves her trying to grab anything in sight and shoving it between her gums. They say you have to have eyes in the back of your head to be a parent to a little one, and I can see what they mean. It's just a shame my husband's eyes are closed because if I hadn't been here, his discarded bottle lid might have resulted in a serious situation and a trip to A & E.

'Look out here,' I say, trying to draw Tuppence's attention away from the items on the table and more towards the sights passing by on the other side of the train window. But any interest my daughter had in watching the world go by through the glass quickly fizzled out ten minutes after we departed the capital, and it's been tricky keeping her entertained ever since.

Even trickier without a certain someone's help.

But while Tuppence has no interest in looking out of the window, I glance at the glass and when I do, I can just about see my reflection staring back at me. It's only faint, but I can still make out my black hair that is full of knots, my sleepy eyes that desperately need rest and my make-up-free face because which new mum has time to beautify herself? If I could, I'd book a haircut, a manicure and a facial, not because I'm vain but just so I might actually look and feel like a thirty-seven-year-old woman again rather than some fatigued husk of a person, shuffling through the days with a baby under one arm and a milk bottle under the other. As it is, I don't have time for anything like that. I mean, I would if Leon would look after Tuppence while I went out by myself and had a break, but he gets flustered far quicker than I do when left alone with her, so it's actually less stressful for me if I just stay.

Leon hasn't had any such challenges in maintaining his appearance since becoming a parent. He is currently sporting a fresh trim to his short black hair, and the muscles poking out from the sleeves of his t-shirt prove that he hasn't missed too many gym sessions since becoming a dad either. I know I need to be firmer with him and carve out some 'me time' rather than let him have it all, but that's just another argument for another day, and there have been enough of those lately for me to feel like it's time for a day off.

As the train slows further and Stirling station comes into view, I decide to wake up my sleeping husband so he can help me prepare to disembark, as leaving a train is not quite as simple as it once was now that we have a baby in tow.

'Say wakey, wakey, Daddy,' I tell Tuppence, and even though she is still far too young to be able to speak, it's more a way of me making the end of Leon's nap a little fun for us all. I could be mean and startle him awake, but I'll try and be kind. But it doesn't seem like it's worked because rather than smile at me or his daughter as he opens his eyes, my husband simply runs a hand over his face and reaches for the last of his water.

I think about telling him about how he could have replaced his bottle lid before his nap rather than leave it on the table for his daughter to grab and potentially choke on, but decide against it at the last second. This is the beginning of our holiday, and I can't let it start with a disagreement that might eventually spill over into an argument. It's arguing that has led us here and made us feel this trip is necessary. I'm not saying the future of our entire marriage hinges on this four-night break we are taking, but the only reason I'm not saying that is because it's frighteningly close to being true.

Leon and I have our problems.

But right now, our problem is getting off this train in time before it leaves for the next station.

No sooner has the train come to a stop in Stirling, Leon and I are out of our seats because we know we need to move quickly. But there's only so much I can do in a fast fashion when I'm holding a baby, so I'm relying on my husband to do a lot of the work, and while I use one hand to grab my suitcase while holding Tuppence tight to my chest with the other, Leon grabs his bag as well as the pram and the backpack full of our baby's things. Clothes. Nappies. Toys. Wipes.

Bottles. Milk. Packing with a little one is not straightforward, and while I've never been one to travel light myself, my girl seems to have accumulated more essentials than me, despite her tender age.

'Come on!' Leon cries in frustration as he tries to manoeuvre both the pram and two of our bags down the aisle, but it wouldn't be an easy task even if he wasn't hungover.

'Put the rucksack on your back,' I tell him, suggesting a way that might make his life easier, but he just keeps huffing and puffing and does it his way, which is inevitably less productive.

I apologise as Leon accidentally catches another passenger's leg with the edge of the pram, before he lets out another deep sigh when a person in front of him inadvertently blocks his way with a piece of their own luggage.

A quick glance through the windows tells me that many of the passengers disembarking here in Stirling are already off the train, and when I see a conductor preparing to put a whistle in his mouth, I fear that we might not make it off in time before we're on the move again.

'Hurry up!' I say to Leon, not that he can go any faster than he already is, and rather predictably, he doesn't take too kindly to me rushing him when he's trying his best.

Tuppence starts crying then, clearly sensing something is wrong in that way that babies seem to be able to do, or maybe she's just upset because she's heard Mummy raising her voice at Daddy before and is preparing for what usually comes next, which is Daddy raising his voice in return. But that doesn't happen, but only because we're in a very public place, and the middle of a busy train carriage is not the ideal setting for a disagreement. Or maybe it's just because time is of the essence, and talking will not speed anything up here.

I don't quite know how we manage it, but we somehow all make it off the train before it's too late. As the doors close behind us and I let out a sigh of relief on the platform, I see Leon's expression and it's one that tells me he's not as thrilled to be here on holiday with me as I would have hoped.

He looks tired, fed up and like he'd rather be anywhere else but where he is currently.

This is only day one.

Welcome to Stirling, hubs.

2

After a bit of a hassle on the platform with all the bags, we've managed to put Tuppence in her pram and walk away from the station and into the centre of Stirling. Now all we need to do is figure out a way to keep ourselves occupied for the next three hours until we're able to check into the apartment that we are renting during our stay.

'Message the host and see if she'll let us check-in earlier so we can get rid of all these bags,' Leon says to me, clearly as eager as I am to be unburdened from our luggage.

It's not a bad idea, though we might not get the outcome we are hoping for, but I'll try anyway, so we stop walking and I take out my phone to type a message. As Tuppence gurgles away in the pram, Leon looks around the street before telling me he's going to buy some water from the small supermarket a little further down the road. I tell him to grab me a bottle too, though I clearly need it far less than he does, and he walks away, leaving me with the bags and the baby.

Nothing new there, then.

Hi, it's Gabby. My family are staying at your apartment today, and I was wondering if we could check-in earlier than three? It would be great if we could drop our bags, but no problem if not. Looking forward to our stay!

I send my message to the owner of the apartment, and it's the first thing I've sent her since I transferred £400 to secure our booking a couple of weeks ago. But I don't know how long it will take her to see this message, nor if she will reply with good news and say we can get in earlier, so I prepare myself for having to keep our bags with us for the next few hours.

Leon returns with the water, and with no word yet from the host, we have to make a plan.

'We could go and see the castle,' I suggest. 'It's a nice day, so we'd get some good photos.'

'What? Walk all the way up that massive hill with our bags? No chance,' comes the gruff response from my husband before he chugs from his fresh bottle.

To be fair to him, he's probably right that walking up a hill with all our luggage in tow is a bad suggestion, so I look around for another idea.

'We could do a bit of shopping,' I say, watching several pedestrians wandering in and out of shop doorways with bags of their own in hand.

'How about we find somewhere for lunch?' Leon proposes, and when I check the time, I see that it is probably acceptable to go for something to eat now, so I agree, and we start walking to find anywhere that serves food. I calculate that it'll soon be time for Tuppence's next feed as well, so that will work out nicely, and maybe this holiday isn't going to begin as disastrously as I first feared. Leon's mood certainly seems to have improved once I agreed with his plan for lunch, although I wonder if that is only because he's planning on having a beer when we get there.

'What's wrong? We're on holiday,' I bet he'll say if I question why he is drinking again so soon after last night, so I might not even bother. I suppose he could be right, we are on holiday, although the circumstances that have brought us here are hardly normal.

When most families book a vacation, it's usually because they all need a break and are looking forward to getting to spend some quality time together somewhere different to home. But while we do need a break, having become parents this year and dealt with all the craziness that entails over these last six months, a change of scene is not the main reason I booked this trip.

I booked it because it was either this or my marriage was over.

I know that sounds dramatic, but it's true. The way things were going, something had to change, and the quickest way I could think to create that change was to suggest something that would snap us out of the routine that was threatening to derail our marriage. It's the routine that would see Leon and I go through the whole day barely saying two words to each other, him working away in his home office upstairs, me trying to keep Tuppence entertained in the playroom downstairs, and even when our little girl was put to bed, conversation was still at a minimum. I'd discuss our child's developmental milestones with him, and he would nod along and pretend he'd read the books I'd recommended he read before our baby was born, before I'd ask him about his day. He'd then mumble a few things about how nothing exciting ever happens to a computer programmer like him, and that would be about it. We'd spend the last hour or so of the day mindlessly watching something on television that both of us were too tired to actually pay attention to before we'd retire to bed, and lately, our beds were separate.

Sometimes, I'd suggest Leon go in the spare room so he could get a better night's rest before work than he would if he was in the same room as Tuppence, who woke regularly in the night, although only for cuddles, not feeds, thankfully. Other times, Leon would suggest it, telling me he'd love to be in the main bedroom with me but he had an early morning call and needed to be fresh for that. But really, both of us were quite relieved we'd get to spend the night sleeping apart because it meant less time having to pretend like we were still a functioning couple.

So how did our marriage end up like this? It certainly hadn't started this way. We used to be great together, always laughing, having fun, both of us with lots to say to the other and neither one ever contemplating a night apart if we could help it. But then I got pregnant, although it certainly wasn't Tuppence's fault that our relationship became strained. We both wanted a child, and we were both thrilled when we found out we were expecting one. It wasn't my fault either because I did everything an expectant mother should do during my pregnancy. I rested, took my vitamins, avoided raw meat and alcohol and read as many books as I could about sleep routines, wake windows, feeding schedules and ways to stimulate a newborn child so they develop just right. Tuppence did what she was supposed to do too, coming along almost on her due date and giving me few problems during her birth, just like I did what I was supposed to do after that -

loving her from the second I saw her and adjusting my life to ensure every decision I made was with her optimum health foremost in my mind.

But somebody didn't play their part.

Somebody was at fault.

Somebody did their best to mess it all up.

It was just as I was entering the third trimester with Tuppence when I discovered Leon's penchant for sex workers, although my husband wouldn't call them that. He'd say they were 'webcam girls', as if that makes it any better. Whatever they are called, and I've called them all sorts of names ever since I found out that Leon was paying to watch them, it is still something that a wife doesn't expect to have to put up with in a marriage. Okay, so he might not have actually slept with any of those women. He hasn't even been in the same room as them. But he was subscribed to a website on which he could watch them offer their services, and by services, I mean they would gyrate around half naked on a bed and titillate their viewers who would message in with words of encouragement.

I caught Leon 'watching' one of these webcam girls late one night when I got up to use the bathroom. At that time, I was 27 weeks pregnant, meaning my bladder was the size of a pea. I was also feeling bloated, sleep-deprived and anxious, the initial joy of expecting a baby having worn off weeks before, and now, all the anxieties of what was really happening had been starting to hit hard. It was a time when I needed my partner the most for support to get me through the last few months of my pregnancy. I thought he was doing just that when he offered to sleep in the spare bedroom so that I had more space in the main bed for me and my uncomfortable bump. Unfortunately, that suggestion extended to Leon repaying me by using the privacy of the spare bedroom to take pleasure in women who were not his wife.

He told me it wasn't what it looked like, and he pleaded that he wasn't cheating. It was just silly nonsense, he said, stupid male stuff, no harm done, apparently. Yet he wasn't the one who felt hurt by catching his partner enjoying somebody else, and hurt I was. I was offended too, as well as disgusted to learn my husband paid £39.99 to subscribe to see these women in action.

I told him to get out of the house, before he told me that I was overreacting. I started screaming then before Leon told me I had to calm down because getting worked up might harm our unborn baby. Annoyingly, he was probably right about that, so I did force myself to calm down, but only for the baby and nobody else, and because of that, Leon stayed in the home. He then proceeded to spend the rest of my pregnancy making up for his actions by doting on me and trying to prove it really was just something stupid and not worth ruining a marriage over. Of course, I still felt hurt, but I had something big to distract me – literally. My bump grew and grew until Tuppence made her appearance into the world, and at that moment, I thought we could be okay.

Seeing how Leon was with our child during his paternity leave made my heart soften to him again, and the scars of his late night 'webcam sessions' started to heal. At least, they did until he returned to work and suddenly, it was as if everything started going wrong again. He was tired and irritable, just like I was and as all new parents are, but if it had just been the stress of a baby, we could have been fine. But when I found out Leon had gone back to watching the webcam girls, despite vowing he never would, I couldn't believe it.

I told him we were over.

He begged for one last chance.

I looked at our baby and thought I deserved to give her father one more go.

So I booked this holiday.

Looking at Leon as he pushes the pram through the open pub door ahead of me, I wonder if I'm simply delaying the inevitable. The damage between us might already be done, and I'm asking a hell of a lot of Stirling for it to somehow save my marriage. Even Barbados might not be enough for us at this point.

Maybe this is a waste of time and I'll leave Leon after this holiday – leave him to all his women online. Maybe he can go and meet them in person while I raise our child by myself. Or maybe, just maybe, this break might be the thing that keeps us together. I guess time will tell.

It might be just another family holiday.

Or it might end up being our last.

As we entered the pub, I had no idea it would be the latter.

3

We've been in the pub for an hour and in that time, I managed to get Tuppence to fall asleep in her pram so that Leon and I could eat our lunch far easier than if she had been awake during it. But she's up again now and it's time for her to be fed, and guess who's on milk duty? I'll give you a clue. It's not my husband, the guy currently standing at the bar and talking to one of the locals about the state of Scottish football while they both order themselves another beer.

'Good girl,' I say to my daughter after I manage to get her to do another burp, before I put the bottle teat back to her lips and she begins to consume yet more milk again. I feel a little sorry for her because she's mostly been on nothing but milk since birth, although her diet has become a little more varied in the last couple of weeks with the start of weaning and the introduction of some vegetables, or 'mush' as Leon calls it. But it's hardly going well, and she's got a way to go before she gets to have a more balanced diet, though she hasn't missed much by not eating the food they serve here. I ordered the fish and chips, but it wasn't quite as nice as it sounded on the menu, the chips arriving lukewarm and soggy. As for the size of the seafood part of my meal, I've seen bigger goldfish. Nevertheless, I eat it all, hungry and figuring this wasn't the kind of establishment that employed a Michelin-starred chef, anyway. Leon had the burger and he said it was alright, but he's no food critic, which might be for the best because I'm no chef myself.

As I continue to feed Tuppence while Leon sets the world to rights at the bar, it only feels like one of us is on holiday so far. But I get a break from my familiar feelings of frustration when I see a woman my age enter the pub pushing a pram of her own and as she takes a seat at the table next to me, she shows me a warm smile.

'Feeding time too, hey?' she asks me as her warm eyes regard both me and my baby, and I smile and nod my head before watching her get out a milk bottle and prepare to start a feed of her own.

She has a little girl with her who looks to be the same age as Tuppence, give or take a week or two, and as that feed gets underway, I feel like I might as well make conversation, not just because the woman keeps looking at me and smiling but because it's not as if I have anybody else to talk to at the moment.

'She's gorgeous. What's her name?' I ask as I pull a silly face at the baby at the next table.

'Lexi,' comes the reply from her mother. 'I decided to go with something a bit more modern.'

'It's a lovely name,' I say, meaning it.

'And who is this little one here?' I'm asked then as the woman starts cooing over my baby.

'This is Tuppence,' I reply with a grin, proud of my beautiful little girl. 'She's six months old. I'm guessing Lexi is similar?'

'Yeah, six and a half,' comes the reply from Lexi's mum. 'I don't know where the time has gone.'

'Me neither,' I admit. 'It's all a bit of a whirlwind, isn't it?'

'Sure is. I'm Raquel, by the way.'

My fellow mother breaks off from the feed for a moment then to offer her hand and I do the same, shaking her hand before giving my own name.

'Gabby,' I say, before asking the next obvious question. 'So, is she your first?'

'She is,' Raquel replies. 'Although I almost had another one just like her. Lexi was a twin. Sadly, we lost her sister just before birth.'

'Oh my god, I'm so sorry,' I say, wishing I hadn't even asked now because that sounds terrible, and I didn't mean to make this poor woman recount such a bad memory.

'It's okay. I mean, it's not okay, but I'm getting there,' Raquel admits. 'Lexi keeps me busy, and I've not really had time to process it all yet, but maybe that's a good thing.'

I nod my head and show my sympathy again, feeling like I'm not sure what to say next. Fortunately, Raquel speaks first.

'Tuppence is beautiful,' she says whilst admiring my daughter, and while I agree, when I look down at my girl, I see her cheeks are covered in milk and she has gone rather red.

Wiping her face with a muslin and checking she hasn't done a dirty nappy again, I figure I'm okay for now, which is good because I doubt this pub has the finest baby-changing facilities in the world.

'Is she your first?' Raquel asks, and I nod my head.

'Yeah, and possibly my only,' I reply.

'Oh, you don't want another one?'

'It's complicated,' I say before I glance at the bar and when I do, Raquel seems to realise what I'm hinting at as she looks at Leon too.

'The father?' she asks.

'Yep, that's him,' I reply. 'As you can see, he's much more adept with a pint of beer in his hand than he is with a bottle of milk.'

'I'm sure he tries,' Raquel says, but I just roll my eyes at that to show her just how hard he does.

'What about you? Are you going to have another, or is it too early to say?' I ask before realising I've probably just put my foot in it again by asking such a question after what this woman has already been through. But Raquel doesn't seem flustered by my enquiry at all.

'Oh yes, I want another,' she says confidently. 'A girl, ideally. The sister Lexi was meant to have.'

That sounds sweet, I suppose, if a little laced with melancholy and also adding pressure to the next child, who might end up being a boy. But I don't say anything and because I don't, I notice Raquel is staring intently at Tuppence once again.

I suddenly get the feeling that me being here with my daughter in such close proximity to a mother with her history might be a little weird, so I make a point of checking my phone, if only to break up our conversation. When I do, I see that I have a missed call and a text from Kelly, the owner of the townhouse we've booked, and the message carries good news.

We can check-in now.

That might be just the excuse to extricate myself from this slightly awkward situation, and as I see Raquel is still staring at my daughter, I make my excuses and prepare to leave.

'It was lovely to meet you,' I say, and Raquel seems sad to see me go, or rather she seems sad to see Tuppence going because that's who she's staring at.

'You too,' she replies, before I call out to Leon to come and give me some help with our things.

He ignores my first attempt at getting his attention but knows better than to ignore my second, and as he returns to our table, I see he still has half of his pint left. Too bad because I'm ready to leave, Tuppence is starting to get cranky, and we can finally check into the place we've paid good money to be at this week.

'Come on, let's go,' I tell my husband, and he quickly finishes his beer because he couldn't just leave it unfinished, could he?

I put Tuppence back in her pram as Leon grabs our bags, but before we can exit, Raquel stands up with Lexi and leans over the pram.

'Goodbye, Tuppence, it was lovely to meet you,' she says before holding her daughter's hand and making it wave as if the little girl is saying goodbye too.

It's cute, I suppose, and Leon laughs at it, but I'm also aware this is a woman who is grieving her child's lost sister, and for some reason, she seems quite enamoured with my baby, so I just smile and begin pushing the pram away.

'Bye, Gabby. Nice to meet you,' Raquel calls after me, and I say it was nice to meet her too before I get outside the pub.

'Made a new friend, did we?' Leon asks me as we head along the street in the direction of our accommodation, but I just ask him the same, referring to the guy he was chatting about football with at the bar.

'You know, it would have been nice if you helped me out with the feed,' I add, but Leon seems confused, as if he thinks it's a one-person job, so what could he have possibly done to assist?

I just shake my head at him before checking my phone, upon which is the map that is guiding me to the place we are staying for the next four nights.

I hope it's as nice as the photos when we get there.

I need it to be good.

That's because so far, this holiday hasn't quite gone to plan.

4

It's a relief to see that the accommodation looks exactly as advertised and now we're in it, we can begin to enjoy our stay.

I chose this place for several reasons, the most important one being practicality of hosting a six-month-old child. That meant not having several staircases to carry all our paraphernalia up, or tiny bedrooms that were too small to fit a travel cot in. But after ticking those boxes, I also wanted somewhere that looked good because this holiday wasn't just for Tuppence but her parents too. I needed somewhere that Leon and I could relax in together, somewhere that made us feel comfortable and, hopefully, somewhere that could help us rekindle our spark and put our troubled past firmly to bed. I know a pile of bricks can't work miracles, but, then again, some interior designers aren't far off miracle workers with what they end up producing, and this place is certainly proving that.

An eye-catching townhouse in the centre of Stirling is our base for this trip and after relieving ourselves of our luggage and leaving Tuppence in her pram for a moment, Leon and I quickly explored the premises. The first part of the property we saw was the large living area where a large TV screen is flanked by a pair of plush sofas and behind one of those is a bookcase that houses all manner of riveting reads. We recognised that the handcrafted, wooden coffee table between the sofas would make a useful place to set down a glass of wine or two during one of our planned movie nights while Tuppence slept, and there's even a fireplace to add more of a cosy feel to the room.

Satisfied with where we could spend the first part of our evening, Leon and I went to explore the room where we would go for the latter part of it, and as we entered the master bedroom, we were immediately drawn to the super king-sized bed. Even with Tuppence sleeping in the cot beside it, it was clear we'd most likely get a good night's rest in here, aided by the black-out blinds on the windows.

All the floors in the townhouse are wooden but rather than feel cold, it gives the place a rustic feel. The kitchen is a good size, perfect for what we'll need it for, which is mainly preparing Tuppence's bottles because we plan to eat out for our meals. After dropping a few bags in the second, smaller bedroom, we check out the bathroom. I know Leon couldn't care less about this room and would be happy with a basic toilet, shower and sink, but I place great importance on this part of the property because it's one part that I don't want to be shabby. But it's far from that, and as well as there being a big bath for Tuppence, there is a large walk-in waterfall shower for the adults to enjoy.

'We could try out that shower together when Tuppence is asleep,' Leon cheekily suggested to me as we left the bathroom and returned to our baby, but I ignored that idea, not because I'm a prude but because it's been a very long time since my husband and I were intimate with each other. I can't blame that on his dalliance with webcam girls, though, because it had started before. Maybe I can blame it on our baby, but that wouldn't be very fair on her, though it is a fact that my pregnancy was when the physical side of our relationship fizzled out.

Can we figure it out here?

Do I even want to?

I try not to dwell on that too much for the time being and focus on unpacking and once that is done, I check the time. But just before I can say what I'm about to, Leon has an idea.

'I might go and buy a few beers to stock the fridge up,' he says, pulling out his wallet from his jeans pocket and checking how much cash he has in there.

'Not yet you aren't,' I reply quickly. 'It's time to start Tuppence's bedtime routine.'

Leon looks surprised, as if he'd forgotten the early evenings can't be what they used to be like. But I don't forget, mainly because one deviation from our daughter's routine can mean a very tough evening all around.

'We'll take her out in the pram for her fifteen-minute nap and some fresh air. Then we'll come back and put her in the bath,' I say, though I shouldn't have to because it's the same routine every night. 'Then you can feed her, and I'll get her to sleep after that. Cool?'

Leon doesn't look like it's cool, but he knows better than to say anything, and instead of preparing to go and buy beer, he helps me take Tuppence outside in her pram.

Back out on the streets of Stirling, the feeble winter sun is beginning to set, and the temperature is dropping quickly, but Tuppence is warm enough beneath two blankets. I'm just as snug in my winter coat, but Leon looks a little chilly in his thin jacket, though he's big enough to dress himself and should know better at his age than to venture out in February without the appropriate attire.

As we walk away from our lovely accommodation and turn onto a street called Buckingham Place, I'm instantly struck by how big the properties here are. This is clearly the affluent part of the city, and that fact has not escaped Leon either.

'Wow, look at these homes,' he says as we pass one large house after another. 'Can you imagine living in one of these?'

I can, actually, because it just so happens that one of my talents in life is visualising myself living in a much bigger house than the one that I currently reside in, and as we keep walking, I'm quickly in full fantasy mode. I can see myself occupying the house to my left, pottering around that kitchen I can see through the window, the one with the huge breakfast bar and the multitude of cookery books on the shelf above the sink. I can also see myself in the lounge area of the next house, the one with the sheepskin rugs over the sofas, as if the heat from the glowing fireplace is not enough. The house after that, the one with twinkling lights in the oak tree in the middle of the front garden, makes me think about being here at Christmas and putting up festive decorations of my own, and the house beyond that makes my imagination run wild when I see the garage has clearly been converted into some kind of outhouse.

The homes are big, the gardens that surround them are bigger and, best of all, it's so quiet here. The only sounds I can hear are the pram wheels trundling over the pavement and the occasional soft breath from Tuppence as she slowly drifts off, and I bet it's even quieter inside the properties. All in all, what a lovely place to live.

'Look at that,' Leon says, pointing something out, and when I follow his finger, I see Stirling Castle aglow on the top of the hill in the distance, bathed in the last of the day's sunlight, and as if these homes didn't have enough, they also have a spectacular view of the medieval centrepiece of this city.

'What do you reckon a house around here costs?' Leon asks me then, but I couldn't even begin to guess.

'More than we could afford,' I reply, sadly, before I'm struck by another sad thought too, and that is that we have even less of a chance of affording one of these houses if my husband is still secretly spending money subscribing to webcam sites in his spare time.

I tell myself not to think like that and try to stay positive, wanting to believe that Leon is being honest with me now and has genuinely stopped that unsavoury hobby of his. Thinking along those lines, I have a go at trying to repair the broken bond between us.

While my husband currently has both hands on the pram, I offer my hand for him to hold, and he removes one of his hands to take it. I give his hand a small squeeze then and he squeezes back, and while it's a very small and simple thing, it makes me feel a little bit better. I'm hoping now that Leon might say something to acknowledge recent events between us or how this moment here is pleasant, anything that would make me feel like he is determined to make this trip a success for us. But he doesn't do that. He says nothing, leaving me to fill what could easily become an awkward silence if I leave it any longer.

'This is nice,' I say, meaning it. 'Getting away with you and Tuppence. I think it's just what we needed.'

Maybe I'm trying too hard, and maybe Leon is the only one out of the pair of us who should really be trying to make things better, but whatever. I'm serious when I say this holiday is make or break for us, which is why it's extremely disappointing when I hear what Leon has to say next.

'Do you think you'll be okay to bath Tuppence yourself when we get back?' he asks me. 'I'm just thinking the shops will probably shut soon, so I better go and get my beers before they do.'

I shake my head at what he's just suggested, not just frustrated that he's happy to abandon me again with our baby but that he's thinking about something as unimportant as his next alcoholic drink while we're supposed to be out here having quality time together.

'I'd prefer it if you stayed back and helped me,' I reply. 'Tuppence would too. You know she loves it when we both bath her.'

'She's six months old. She doesn't know who's bathing her. She doesn't know anything yet.'

'Yes, she does. She recognises our faces. You know she does. She smiles when she sees us.'

'Fine,' Leon says under his breath, and I've obviously got him to agree but begrudgingly.

I'm just about to ask him what he hopes to get out of this holiday, if he's more bothered about getting drunk than spending time with his family, when I notice somebody standing at a window of the house across the road. My eyes were drawn to them because the light is on inside the house, contrasting with the increasing gloominess outdoors. At first, I just presume it's some random resident of this spectacular street, a property millionaire who will never sell because why would they when they live in a house like that? But then I realise that it's not just some random stranger - it's a woman I recognise, and she's holding a baby I recognise too.

It's Raquel and Lexi.

'Isn't that the woman you were talking to in the pub?' Leon asks me, clearly having noticed her too, and I'm not surprised because as we pass directly opposite the house, Raquel remains at the window, looking right back at us.

'Yeah,' I reply, wondering why she is staring at us, and I ponder whether to wave or not. But that seems weird because we only met once and barely know each other, nor did I ever think we'd meet again, so I leave it.

Raquel doesn't wave either, though maybe just because her hands are full carrying her child, and as we pass the house, I look away and tell Leon to do the same.

'What's the problem?' he asks me.

'I don't know. There's something about that woman,' I reply before regretting it because I know Leon will pry for more now. But I don't mention anything else, certainly not the fact that Raquel has a sad backstory to go with her new baby. Instead, I focus on my own child and the fact her nap can't go on too much longer.

'Let's go back,' I say five minutes later, and Leon doesn't disagree, so we turn around and head for our temporary residence again.

When we pass Raquel's house a second time, she is no longer standing at the window.

But it's weird because I still feel like somebody is watching me.

5

As is often the case, bedtime with Tuppence was hard. I know it's not her fault; she's tiny and her circadian rhythm isn't fully developed yet, not to mention the big wide world must seem very frightening to somebody who was safe inside her mother's womb not so long ago. I'm aware getting a baby to sleep and getting them to stay asleep is supposed to be tough, but there are some things that could make it easier.

Like the support of my partner, for one.

However, as he tends to do, Leon drifted out of the bedroom while I was trying to get Tuppence settled in her crib, conveniently disappearing at the crucial part of the day when our baby becomes extra difficult to deal with. He always comes up with some excuse as to why he goes, saying he'll go and tidy up or is just visiting the bathroom, but he rarely returns until I emerge from the bedroom and tell him our baby is at rest. I'd have hoped he'd have volunteered to take over this part of the routine by now and allow me to have an easier evening, and it is only really a one-person job. Just a shame I'm always that one person.

As I sat with Tuppence, cradling her in my arms and shushing her into what I hoped would be a long and restful slumber, I did start to wonder why I am still giving Leon a chance. It was one thing for him to fail me as a husband but to be failing his daughter as a father is on another level. It feels like he sees Tuppence more as just an inconvenience rather than a part of our family now, not that he would ever admit it. But actions speak louder than words. However, by the time I had successfully got our baby to drift off and rest in her crib, I already knew the answer as to why I was still with him.

Right now, it feels like I am doing all this on my own.

But if I left Leon, I really would be by myself.

As I leave the bedroom and enter the living area, it's no surprise to find my husband sitting on the sofa with the television on. Nor is it a surprise to find he has already opened the bottle of red wine he'd almost forgotten he had packed for this trip. He was pleased when he remembered it because it meant he didn't have to venture out to the nearest shop and buy booze, at least not today anyway, and as he sees me walk in, he quickly volunteers to pour me a glass.

That's Leon all over. Quick to offer me a drink. Slow to offer me support for something meaningful.

As it turns out, a glass of wine would be good right about now, so I accept it and take a seat on the sofa beside my husband. But as usual, it's not long before any thoughts of relaxing are spoiled when I realise that in all the commotion to get Tuppence fed and in bed, I haven't planned anything for our dinner. But that's when Leon actually makes himself useful.

'I've ordered us a pizza,' he says with a grin. 'I found a takeaway menu on the fridge and called while you were in the bedroom. One large cheese and tomato pizza on its way, with a side of garlic bread.'

That's music to my ears, although not necessarily positive news for my waistline, but I thank

Leon for being proactive, and maybe all is not as doom and gloom as it seems in my world. I am also sleep-deprived, so that could be warping my view of things a little bit. Maybe my husband isn't actually that bad. He certainly could be worse. He could be out drinking now rather than here with me. He could be the kind of guy who expects his dinner on the table rather than sorts it himself. He could be the type of father who is totally absent from his child's life. And he could have actually slept with one of those women rather than just watch them online.

Telling myself things are okay, I snuggle down beside my man, and he gives the top of my head a kiss as we watch some easy-going quiz show presented by a famous comedian who has clearly cashed in on this job because it's easier than travelling the country telling jokes to large crowds every night. By the time it finishes, our food has arrived, and once we're tucking in, my mood improves further. My outlook gets even rosier as I check the baby monitor several times and see that Tuppence is sleeping soundly, and this might just end up being a great first night of our holiday after all.

As we eagerly consume our pizza and garlic bread, we discuss our plans for tomorrow, and we quickly agree that a trip to the castle is a must, made much easier now that we won't be carrying our bags with us. I also suggest a little shopping, which Leon agrees to, and because of that, I make sure to tell him that there will be time in the day for him to have a beer or two along the way. It's all very normal and nice and I guess no different to how other couples would spend an evening away with a baby, but things take a turn when I stupidly decide to talk about something more serious than tomorrow's plans.

'We're okay, aren't we?' I ask, possibly sounding a little needy, but if a woman can't be needy with her partner, who can she be like that with?

'Yeah, of course,' Leon says while eating his dinner.

'I'm serious,' I go on, forcing him to actually listen to me and not just reply with half-hearted responses. 'I need to know that things are back to normal for us. And eventually going to get better.'

Leon stops eating then and looks a little annoyed.

'You promised you wouldn't keep going on about the past,' he says.

'I'm not talking about the past.'

'You're hinting at it. Why can't we just enjoy tonight and focus on the future?'

'Because I need to know that we have a future.'

'What's that supposed to mean?'

'I mean, I need to know that you're going to keep working at being better for me and Tuppence. And I definitely need to know before we think about giving her a brother or a sister.'

Leon looks like the pizza is the last thing on his mind now, so at least I know I have his full attention. However, he doesn't look thrilled by this topic of conversation.

'What are you saying? That I'm a bad father and you don't know whether or not to risk having another child with me?'

'No, of course not!'

'Then what?'

'I'm just saying, I can't put up with anything else, Leon. I'm not just talking about what you've done in the past, I am talking about the future. I need you to be more present, more willing to help. To show me that your family is your priority.'

It might not be sensible, but I'm spilling all my fears out for Leon to hear and in the process, drowning out the noise from the TV, as well as the satisfaction we were getting from our food, which is now sitting untouched.

'What do you want me to say? That I won't use those webcam girls again? That I'll try and be a better father and husband? Because I've said all those things before, Gabby, so I don't know why you're making me say it again.'

'Maybe because I'm not sure I believe it,' I reply before quickly regretting it.

Leon looks surprised at my admission, but I can't take it back, and now it's out there, at least I won't go home from this holiday with any regrets. I've said my piece. Now what does my husband have to say in response?

'You should believe it,' he tells me, looking me right in the eye and even taking my hand to emphasise his point. 'I'm trying to do better, and I will do better.

Just work with me a little. I'm not perfect and never will be, but I do try.'

While I've been honest, at least Leon is being that way too, and I guess I can't take issue with him being open with me, so I smile and give his hand a squeeze.

'Our pizza's getting cold,' I remind him, changing the subject and also letting him know that I'm happy enough with his answers, so we both know where we stand.

We finish our meal and the rest of the night goes well, particularly for Leon, who finishes the wine in the bottle. I stopped at one glass because that's usually my limit these days anyway, but Leon had plenty more, and that's probably why he got frisky with me as I turned off the TV and suggested we go to bed.

We share a kiss which quickly feels like it could turn into much more, and it's clear he wants to go further, but I'm not quite there yet. I'm still wounded by what I caught him doing and that's why I haven't been able to sleep with him since, as well as the fact that I'm still self-conscious about my post-partum body. That's why I separate my lips from his before things get too hot and heavy, though predictably, Leon wants to carry on.

'Maybe tomorrow night,' I say with a wink and that should be enough, but Leon just looks grumpy now, and as we creep into the bedroom where Tuppence sleeps and prepare to climb into bed nearby, I am wondering if I should have just let him have his fun out there in the living room. Maybe that would be the best thing for our relationship. Or maybe not. It's just sex. We should be built on firmer ground than that.

But are we?

I can't ask Leon because we need to be quiet with Tuppence so close to us.

I also can't ask him because he's just put his headphones in and is watching some football highlights on his phone.

Goodnight, then.

6

Our second day in Stirling was eventful but for all the wrong reasons. Leon and I were woken at three o'clock in the morning by the sound of Tuppence's cries and despite changing and feeding her before putting her back down again, neither of us managed to get back to sleep. By the time we both gave up and got out of bed, we opened the curtains to see torrential rain falling over this part of Scotland. Nothing new there, perhaps, but in this case, not what the weather forecasters had predicted for this week.

Needing a new plan because a very wet walk uphill to the castle didn't sound much fun, we figured we'd wander around the indoor shopping centre and at least stay dry that way. Of course, Leon quickly grew bored of that, and it wasn't long until we were in a pub again. We did a little more shopping after lunch, a lunch that was interrupted by several nappy changes, but it was always bound to be hard work browsing for things with a pram and a tutting husband in tow, and I eventually conceded and said we'd head back to the house.

On the way there, I saw Raquel again. She was pushing her own pram down the street and there were a couple of shopping bags in the basket underneath it, suggesting she had chosen to spend today in the same way I had. We actually made eye contact at one point, and I wondered if she was going to walk over and say hello to me. I actually wouldn't have minded that either because Leon was getting on my nerves again, so having another adult to converse with for a short time would have been quite welcome. But she didn't come over to chat, nor did she wave, much like when I passed her house last night and saw her standing at the window. I presume she recognised me, but either she didn't feel like we were close enough to talk again or she simply couldn't be bothered to re-engage with me. Then again, I didn't try either, so I've been just as anti-social as her.

I did tell Leon about her, though, her sad story of the child she lost, meaning the joy of giving birth was tempered somewhat by a tragedy, and he was sympathetic. He also glanced back at Raquel as she walked away, a sad look on his face as if he couldn't imagine what she had been through and was almost glad he didn't have to, either. That's the thing with my husband, he seems like a typical bloke, all football, beer and bad jokes, but he has a sensitive side, and I saw that he was visibly moved when I told him what Raquel had lost.

If only he showed that side more often, but it didn't take long for normal service to resume, and as another evening approached, the pressure of Tuppence's bedtime routine threatened to derail us once more. That's why I suggest we take a break from each other.

'Are you okay to take Tuppence for a quick walk?' I ask him as we return to our accommodation. 'She should nap, but don't let her have too long. Be back here in half an hour.'

'What are you doing?' Leon asks, as if I'm getting rid of him and the baby so I can put my feet up and do nothing.

'There are six used milk bottles that need washing and a bedroom floor full of clothes that need tidying, so don't worry, I'll be busy too.'

Leon nods his head before pushing Tuppence away in her pram, and I see him heading in the direction of the picture-perfect streets we wandered around at this time yesterday.

'Remember, not too long!' I call after him and he waves to let me know he understands.

I go inside then and get to work, washing, tidying and maximising every spare second I have until my child returns. But her returning soon becomes a problem because despite Leon being under strict instruction to have her back in half an hour, thirty minutes ticks by, and there is no sign of either of them.

I presume he's only a couple of minutes away so get back to being busy, but when I see it's been fifty minutes, I get annoyed and decide to call him. He knows better than to let Tuppence nap for this long so late in the day, and I'm just about to remind him of it. Unfortunately, I can't do that because he doesn't pick up his phone, and as it reaches an hour since we parted, I'm downright furious with him.

He can put Tuppence to bed tonight and see what hard work he has just made for himself then, I think, shaking my head. *He can see how long it will take her to fall asleep now, and I bet he'll regret giving her that long nap when he's still in the bedroom at nine o'clock trying to hush her cries.*

There's a slightly sadistic part of me that secretly hopes Tuppence will be a nightmare this evening because Leon will suffer more that way, though he'll suffer plenty before then when he eventually gets back and I demand to know what has taken him so long. But as time goes on and I see it has now been one hour and fifteen minutes since Leon left with our baby, my anger starts to subside, and worry begins to set in.

Surely he wouldn't still be walking for this long?

What if something has happened to them?

Are they okay?

Or is my family under threat?

Paranoia quickly replaces anger, and now I'm fretting that something awful has befallen the two people that matter most to me in the world. Have they been struck by a car? It is dark out there; maybe Leon was crossing a street - an unfamiliar street - and a driver didn't see him. That is a terrifying thought, but I try to stay sane and tell myself that's not what has happened.

Leon and Tuppence will be the next people at my door, not two sombre police officers with a sad tale to report.

Once I've calmed down about that, I start to wonder if rather than an accident, my husband's prolonged absence with our daughter is planned. What if he's mad at me? I might have been a little overbearing. Has he got frustrated or overwhelmed or confused and now he's taken our child to try and get some space from me?

Is he in a pub? Or is he considering leaving me like I've considered leaving him?

If so, what if he's simply had enough and caught the train back to Edinburgh with our baby on board?

No, don't be stupid, Gabby. That's an even more ridiculous thought than imagining the two of them lying in the roadside while a distressed driver calls 999. Leon hasn't left me, and he certainly hasn't taken Tuppence with him. Even if he did think we should break up, something I might be inclined to agree with by the end of this holiday, he wouldn't separate me from her.

He's not that cruel.

Flawed but not spiteful.

So where the hell are they?

I hear movement at the front door a moment later and race to open it, eager to see if my family have returned and when I see that they have, I'm overcome with relief. But only for a moment because in the absence of any valid explanation as to why they are late, I quickly get annoyed at my husband.

'Where have you been? You've been gone for ages!' I cry, and Leon does look a little sheepish, so I hope he has a good excuse. Did he get lost out there in the dark? That would be irritating, but he is dopey enough to do such a thing.

Alas, not even his stupidity can save him.

'Sorry, I was listening to a podcast and lost track of time,' he says as if that's fine. 'It's okay. She didn't sleep the whole time. She woke up a while ago, so no harm done. I'm sure she'll go down just fine shortly.'

Lost track of time?

No harm done?

Sure she'll go down just fine?

I'm not happy about any of this, but what can I do? Have a shouting match with Leon right here on the doorstep and make this even worse? Better to just get Tuppence inside and get her bathed as quickly as possible so we can try and salvage some semblance of her usual routine.

'We'll talk about this later,' I say to him, which is an ominous thing for any husband to hear, and as I take Tuppence from her pram, I'm hoping he is nervous for the conversation we will have later. Whether he is or not, he doesn't say, and the pair of us work through the routine until Tuppence is in her sleepsuit and snuggled in her crib.

It doesn't actually take as long to do as I'd feared, so Leon has been lucky there, but not that lucky because I still feel like venting some of my frustration to him, wanting to know why he so blatantly ignored me earlier and kept our baby out late, but before I can do that, I notice something.

It's as I'm folding one of Tuppence's outfits that I make a cursory glance out of the window and when I do, I see somebody standing out on the street underneath one of the many streetlights. It's a woman with a pram, and I already sense it is Raquel before I fully recognise her.

She's looking right at this place, as if she knows who is inside it.

Does she know I'm here?

Why would she even care if I am?

It's a little strange, so I decide that the best thing to do in the circumstances is give her a wave. At least if she waves back, I could tell myself nothing stranger has occurred than just her passing by and catching sight of me in the window.

But she isn't passing by, she is just standing out there opposite me.

And when I wave, she doesn't do anything that makes me feel better about that.

She doesn't wave back to me.

She simply keeps staring.

7

Raquel moved on not long after I waved at her, perhaps because she had been seen out there or maybe because she had seen enough from her point of view. Whatever her reason for looking at this property, and for choosing not to wave back at me, I doubt I'll ever know it.

Maybe it's better if I don't.

But seeing her out there, as well as recalling the way she was looking at Tuppence when we first met in that pub, has me feeling unsettled all night, which is why I choose to go to bed earlier, so I can lie beside my baby and keep an eye on her. Leon doesn't seem too bothered that I prefer bed over an evening with him on the sofa and is in a surprisingly cheerful mood considering he must know that I'm mad at him. However, I haven't vented at him about him being late earlier, having decided to let that one go, nor have I told him that I saw Raquel outside watching us. I presume she saw him pushing Tuppence's pram through the doorway earlier and that's how she knew where we were staying.

Or did she follow him back here?

Whatever the reason, I feel like I'll stay closer than usual to my baby for the rest of my time in Stirling, just in case Raquel appears again and gives me the creeps. I did ask Leon where he went for his walk, curious to know if he did frequent Buckingham Place again, and he eventually admitted that he had gone there, though only after some grumbling about why I needed to know his every movement. He then offered to sleep in the spare bedroom, saying he might snore after a few beers, and I couldn't be bothered to disagree with him.

With the bed to myself, I do sleep better, and I certainly feel better when I wake up after a fairly full night's slumber. Amazingly, Tuppence didn't stir until dawn, and I feel even better when I open the curtains in the living area to see blue skies and dry streets. It looks like a nice day to visit the castle, and once Leon has emerged from the spare room, rubbing his eyes before tidying away the four empty beer cans he forgot to dispose of last night, I tell him the plan.

We're going for a walk.

Once we're out, it feels good to be in the fresh air without the threat of rain looming over us, and it feels even better when Leon pushes the pram all the way up the hill to the castle rather than me. He's sweating by the time we reach the public car park at the top, but considering it's not exactly hot and he's a fit man, I'd say those droplets on his forehead are him sweating out a mild hangover more than anything else.

'It's lovely up here,' I say as I take in the sight of the medieval walls ahead of us before looking both left and right and taking in the rolling green hills that surround this city.

'Yeah, it's great,' Leon says as he gratefully stops pushing the pram and wipes his slightly sweaty brow.

'Let's get some photos,' I suggest, and we do just that, the two of us leaning over Tuppence's pram so she is captured on camera too before we get a couple of selfies of just the pair of us. When I inspect the photos, it looks like we're a very happy couple with one very happy baby, and although that's not quite the truth, in this case, I don't mind.

They say the camera can add ten pounds.

It can also make a troubled marriage look perfect.

However, despite our troubles, Leon seems to be doing his best to put them behind us and has been very cheerful so far. He's not needing any prompting when it's come to doing things for Tuppence, nor has he needed me to remind him about not doing certain things too. He is playing the doting dad, cooing away at our daughter in her pram, who is always looking up at him with wide and loving eyes, seeing her father through the perfect perspective of youth, yet to grow up and learn he isn't quite Superman yet. But it's not just our daughter he's given his attention to. Leon has even found the time to compliment me on my appearance, saying that I look nice as we wandered amongst the walls of the castle. It was a comment that I found hard to take seriously when I heard it, mainly because while I did get more sleep than usual last night, I still feel a long way off looking my best. But my husband has said something to make me feel good and it did cheer me up when I heard it.

After whiling away some time at the top of the hill, we walked back down it and grabbed a quick sandwich from a supermarket before enjoying a gentle stroll beneath the bright blue sky. Finally, after almost half our holiday has passed, I feel like this might be working. Leon and I seem to be doing better and to prove it, he takes hold of my hand as we stroll and shows me a smile before looking down at Tuppence and smiling at her too.

I'm feeling great by the time we get back to our accommodation in the late afternoon, and I'm feeling even better when Leon, utterly uninvited, suggests he takes Tuppence for her last nap of the day in her pram while I go inside and run myself a bath.

'Relax. You deserve it,' Leon says, words that I never thought I'd hear my husband say, but words that I am not going to argue with if I can help it. But that's the thing. Can I help it? After all, this time yesterday, Leon pushing Tuppence around in her pram ended up being an issue.

'Don't worry, I'll have her back on time,' Leon says with a wink, pre-empting my concerns, and I decide to trust him, which is what he deserves after he's been so perfect all day.

I take my husband's advice and run myself a bath while he is out, enjoying every single second that I spend soaking under the soapy suds, and my pleasant day improves even further when I hear the front door opening. Leon is back with Tuppence and he's right on time.

What has gotten into my husband?

Who has he been swapped with?

I don't know, but I also don't care as long as he stays.

'How was your bath?' Leon asks as he sees me emerging from the bathroom with a towel round my torso and another one wrapped around my wet hair.

'Lovely,' I reply before asking him how his walk was.

'Great. She napped for ten minutes and is all ready for her own bath,' Leon says, beaming at our baby, and this day just keeps getting better. So it proves once we get Tuppence to bed for the evening, and once I'm alone with my husband in the living room, I decide to try and pick up where we left off on our first night here.

Leon must be shocked because it takes him a moment to reciprocate my advances, but he soon finds his groove and before we both know it, we've shed our clothes and are lying intertwined on the sofa staring up at the ceiling. Then I decide to say something that I hope he will reciprocate too.

'I love you,' I whisper to him as he strokes my hair.

'I love you too,' he replies right on cue, and just like that, I consider this holiday a success.

If only it had ended there, everything would have been okay.

The nightmare would never have begun.

But it didn't end there.

Not long after we had put our clothes back on and had a bite to eat, Leon mentioned there was a guitarist playing at one of the pubs not far from where we are, and he wondered if he might be able to get out for a beer to listen to some of the music. Having behaved flawlessly all day, I told him that I was happy to stay behind with Tuppence while he went out, and as he kissed me goodbye, I told him to be quiet when he got back. I also told him that I loved him again. He replied with the same.

Then he left, and after watching an hour of television, I went to bed, crawling underneath the duvet and checking on Tuppence in her crib before laying my head on my pillow and closing my eyes.

It felt like the end to the perfect day and in many ways it was.

I didn't know it then but as I drifted off to sleep beside my baby, it would be the last time I would achieve such a restful state for a very, very long time. That's because by the time the following day was over, my life, and the lives of several other people in this Scottish city, would never be the same again.

8

The fourth and final full day of our holiday began with me walking into the living area to find Leon asleep on the sofa.

Having woken just before dawn to the sound of Tuppence wanting food, I had checked the pillow next to me and been startled to find my husband had not slept beside me. Panicking, I looked at my phone to see if he had tried to call me at any point over the last several hours, afraid something bad had happened to him after he had gone out and he was in a hospital somewhere needing his wife and daughter to come and visit him. But there were no missed messages or calls, and after I had scooped Tuppence out of her crib, I rushed around the house to see if there was any sign of the man I married.

When I found him sleeping on the sofa, I was relieved for all of two seconds until he stirred from his slumber at the sound of us entering. That was when I realised that he hadn't just slept in here to be considerate to his family and avoid waking us up when he got in last night. He had slept in here because he had clearly had far too much to drink and was now suffering greatly for it.

'Urgh, what time is it?' Leon mumbles as he rubs his eyes and looks at me like I'm mad for being up at this hour.

'It's six o'clock and your daughter needs changing and feeding,' I say, in no mood to pander to his hangover as I place Tuppence down on her mat and reach into the bag of nappies.

'What time did you get in last night?' I ask Leon as I undress our daughter, but he doesn't have a confident answer to that question.

'Midnight, maybe,' he mutters, but I can tell when he's lying, more so these days than I used to be able to, so I just shake my head and assume it was at least one o'clock before he came through the front door.

'Have a lot to drink?' I ask, a stupid question but why not make my hungover husband feel a little worse for his stupidity?

'I guess so,' he replies, not even trying to pretend like he was sensible, and that's something I suppose.

'Let me guess, you're not going to be much help to me today, are you?' I ask him then, wondering if he'll give me just as honest an answer to that question and surprisingly, he does.

'I need to go to bed,' he tells me before getting off the sofa and shuffling out of the room, looking pale, dehydrated and useless to me.

I change Tuppence's nappy before feeding and playing with her, but after a couple of hours, there is no sign of Leon returning. Gritting my teeth, I think about going into the bedroom, flinging the duvet off him and reprimanding him for undoing all his good work yesterday by ruining today. But I decide to give him another half hour in the futile hope that he might surface by then and be in somewhat of a suitable state.

To kill the time while Leon sleeps and Tuppence lies on her playmat and stares at a multicoloured buzzy bee toy, I use my phone to search online. I'm curious as to how much those big houses on Buckingham Place are, the ones I walked past with Leon and Tuppence and particularly the one I saw Raquel staring out of the window from. I guess they're worth a lot, but it's always nice to put an actual figure on things, isn't it?

Using one of my favourite websites, I type in the name of the street in question, and it instantly shows me all the houses on it and the last time they were sold. I can see the price they went for in that sale too, although when I look at the various homes on the exclusive street, I can see there hasn't been a sale for a while. The last one seems to be four years ago when one of the properties, a six-bed home, sold for £1.1 million. I assume it's worth more now, which is slightly frightening, although not for the current owners. The cheapest four-bed on the street is almost £700,000, which is still a huge amount of money. It's well out of our price range, hundreds of thousands of pounds out, but there are far wealthier people out there than me who I'm sure would be happy to go house-hunting around these parts. You get what you pay for, and I'm sure plenty of people have been happy to pay their money to live somewhere like Buckingham Place, although the lack of recent sales suggests that once a family gets in, they stay, which probably only drives up the prices even more when they do come to sell. Raquel is one of those lucky people who has already secured her home and is now holding on to it, and as I have a snoop around on this website for her house, I see that it was purchased seven years ago.

I wonder how she afforded it. She seems to be a single mum, so she might have had a very good job or perhaps inherited a small fortune from a deceased relative. Or maybe she bought the house with somebody else, a husband, perhaps, but they have since separated. If so, she did well to keep the property in the divorce. Then again, I would certainly have fought to keep it too.

Before I know it, I've managed to waste the best part of half an hour, but I have to break off from my nosy internet search when Tuppence becomes bored and cries for my attention. But I'm bored now too and in need of some attention of my own, so I pick up my little girl and carry her into the bedroom with mischief on my mind.

Ignoring Leon's current condition, I tell him that his daughter is here to see him and put her down right on top of his chest, forcing him to wake instantly and begin daddy duties, lest his child fall off the bed before he can take hold of her. As I hoped he would, Leon looks unprepared for such duties being thrust upon him, but I just smirk before leaving the room and getting myself ready. I know today is going to be hard work, but at least I can take some satisfaction in my husband's stupidity to get blind drunk during a family holiday.

If it's going to be hard for me, I'll make sure it's doubly so for my silly partner.

As to be expected, it takes a long time for us to leave the house and go for a walk, Leon literally dragging his feet when we finally make it out, but he has to push the pram and endure a trip round several shops throughout the morning. We have lunch in a pub, but

Leon must really be in a bad way because he doesn't have a beer, sticking to a lemonade, although he wolfs down his burger in record time. The afternoon sees drizzle falling over Stirling, so we visit an art gallery and museum, as well as the Old Jail, which offers a great insight into prison life back when people were locked up in there. As we wander around the cells, I consider how nice it would be to lock my husband up here for a short while, just to teach him a lesson or two, but he's never actually committed a criminal act.

That's something, I suppose.

The light is quickly fading outside as we leave the jail, and with our last night on holiday looming large, I wonder what it has in store. I never could have envisioned what actually happens, but it started off normally enough. I suggested we push Tuppence around in her pram for her final nap of the day as usual, but Leon quickly told me he needed to go back and have a lie down, so I showed my displeasure by shaking my head and telling him to "just go" and set off with the pram alone.

As Leon goes back for his lie down, I wander towards the large houses on Buckingham Place, eager for one last peek at the affluent homes that I'd spent a little time this morning snooping at online. I wonder if I'll see Raquel again, but there is no sign of her at her window, nor is there anybody else out on the street. The light rain and worsening light is clearly keeping everybody inside, but Tuppence's pram is shielded by a rain cover, and I have my hood up on my coat, so I don't mind being out for a little longer myself.

After passing a couple of properties on either side of Buckingham Place, including Raquel's, I am just considering turning back when I hear an unexpected noise. It's a woman's voice and it's nearby, and although I can't see exactly where it is coming from, I can hear what she is saying.

'Help me!'

The two words are loud enough to hear, but not deafening, and it isn't so much a cry borne out of pain or urgency, just desperation for somebody to come to her aid, whoever she might be.

'Help me, please!'

I hear the voice again and look all around the street but can't see anybody out here with me, so I'm unsure how I can help. But somebody definitely needs assistance, and if only I can find them, I'll be happy to offer it. Then I hear the voice for a third time and when I do, I finally get some sense of where it is coming from.

I think it's coming from the rear of the house that I'm standing right in front of.

'Hello?' I say, calling out to see if I get any response.

'Help me! Quick!'

There it is again, and now I'm convinced it is this house, so I push the pram towards the property, treading upon the driveway and calling out again. The voice that calls back definitely comes from the rear of the house, so I go for the side gate and open it. When I do, I hear the voice again and it's much louder this time, letting me know that I'm definitely getting closer. The only problem is, once the gate is open, I see that there are several bins down the side of the property blocking the route. What that means is that it is going to be very difficult for me to get the pram through.

Realising I can't get down the side of the house with Tuppence with me, I consider what to do. I don't want to leave her, even for a moment, but then I hear the woman's voice again and she sounds hurt.

'Help me! I need help!'

There's only one thing I can do.

I need to help this poor woman, whoever she is.

Making a split-second decision, I leave Tuppence for a moment, safely in her pram, hidden down the side of this house and out of view of anyone who might pass by on the street. I rush down the side of the property, squeezing myself past the numerous bins before arriving in the back garden. But when I get there, all I can make out in the fading light is a large, trimmed lawn, several plant pots and a tall conifer standing proudly against the back fence.

'Hello? Where are you? Are you okay?' I call out to the woman who so desperately needed me a moment ago, but for the first time since I heard her, she doesn't respond to my calls.

'Hello?' I try again, figuring it's worth one more shot because I know I definitely heard somebody down here. But again, there is no response.

Unsure what to do, I figure my best course of action is to return to the pram and then see if I can hear anything else from the front of the house. If not, maybe everything is okay with that woman now, although I could always make a cursory call to the police and ask them to make a check at this address. But first things first, I want to get back to Tuppence, so I hurry back around the bins again until I reach the pram.

That's when I know that something is wrong, after all, because that's when I see that the pram is empty.

My baby is gone.

9

There's a very surreal, almost 'out of body' moment when I think this isn't actually happening and I must be dreaming.

My baby isn't missing. Someone hasn't taken her.

I haven't just lost the most important person in my life.

As my body is flooded with adrenaline and gripped by fear, a million thoughts run through my head in a few split seconds, my brain desperately trying to make sense of this situation and come up with an explanation that differs from the terrifying reality that I surely can't be finding myself in now.

The woman's voice I heard. There was no one there when I checked. That suggests it was all in my head. So it could be a dream, right? People don't just hear voices, and people don't just vanish into thin air in real life. If it was real, there would have been somebody in that back garden when I went to look, and if it was real, Tuppence couldn't have just been taken in such a brief window of time, right?

A warm feeling comes over me for a moment when I realise this must be a dream. So all I need to do now is wake up and it'll be over, and normal service will resume. I'll open my eyes in bed, look to my left and see my baby fast asleep in her crib, where she belongs and where she is safe.

That is about to happen as soon as I wake up.

So wake up, Gabby, and look at your child.
Wake up, Gabby.
WAKE UP!

But peace does not come for me, and I realise this is not a dream. This is actually happening, and the longer I try to pretend it isn't, the further away the person who took my baby is getting.

'Tuppence!' I cry out, my voice piercing through the still dusk air and hopefully sending a shockwave around this seemingly deserted street so that somebody hears it and comes to my aid. Maybe my daughter will hear her mother's voice and let out a cry to let me know where she is. If not, her kidnapper must have heard me, and it might spook them into making a mistake and slipping up from their devious plan.

'Tuppence!'

It has to have been planned, doesn't it? It all happened so fast, how could it be the result of anything but a sinister plot to separate me from my child? The thought that somebody plotted this whole thing is frightening because if they have, they have surely plotted how to get away with it, and that means my chances of seeing my baby again are even less.

'Tuppence!'

Unless it was just opportune. Somebody was passing by, saw a child in a pram and snatched her. I thought I had left her out of view, but maybe I hadn't. So was it just a random act to take her? No prior planning behind it whatsoever - just instinct - crazy, illegal instinct.

So which is it?

A perfectly executed plan or a spur of the moment thing?

I'm not sure which is more terrifying.

'Tuppence!'

Calling my daughter's name is getting me nowhere, so I start running, reaching the middle of the road and looking in all directions, wondering if I'll see a speeding car making a getaway in the distance or perhaps a glimpse of the kidnapper's body darting behind a bush or onto the next street, my frightened baby in their arms. But I see nothing other than parked cars and concrete. Nobody is walking or running or driving.

I'm the only one out here.

How can this be?

Then a thought hits me like a lightning bolt from the darkening sky above.

My baby must still be here somewhere.

I stop looking down the two ends of Buckingham Place and turn my focus on the houses that line it. Is Tuppence in one of these homes? Behind one of these doors? Smuggled away inside by one of these residents?

That makes more sense to me than the alternative, which is that someone escaped from here with her, because they surely wouldn't have had the time. I'd have heard a getaway car, never mind seen one, and if they were on foot and running away, I'd have heard and seen that too. The fact I didn't hear a thing and it all happened so fast must mean the culprit is still very close.

Pre-empting what the kidnapper must want me to do, rather than run down the street and get myself lost in this city trying to find somebody who isn't there, I run to the nearest house and bang on the door. It's the house I just went into the garden of. But when there's no answer, I run to the next one and bang on that door too. I don't know which house might be harbouring my baby, but I'm convinced she's here somewhere, so if I can make enough of a scene and get all these residents out of their homes, then maybe I can find her.

'Tuppence!' I cry again as I bang on a third door, but as of yet, nobody has answered my calls. It's still that time of day when people would be making their way home from work, so maybe a lot of these houses are empty. But somebody must be home. Somebody might have seen what happened.

Or somebody here knows exactly what happened.

It's as I'm running towards the fourth house when the door to the third one flings open, and I hear a voice behind me.

'Are you okay?'

I spin around to see a balding man in his sixties wearing a blazer coated in breadcrumbs and the type of corduroy trousers that my grandad used to wear. He looks confused as to what I am doing, and he also doesn't look like somebody who would steal a baby, but everybody is a suspect here.

'I've lost my baby! She's been taken!' I cry. 'Have you seen her? Have you got her? Where is she?'

My barrage of questions only serves to fluster the man even more and before he can answer any of them, I hear another door opening. It's across the street, and while I haven't banged on that door yet, the homeowner inside has clearly heard all the commotion and come out to see what is going on around this normally quiet neighbourhood.

'Where's my baby? Do you have her?' I wail, rushing towards the second person to leave their home, in this case a woman in her seventies who peers at me through her thin-rimmed spectacles and looks more annoyed than concerned.

'What are you talking about?' she says, her voice much lower than mine, as if raising her voice is beneath her, but I bet she would soon change her mind about that if she had lost her own baby.

'Somebody took my daughter!' I cry. 'She was in her pram over there and now she's gone. Please, you have to help me! She must be here somewhere! Somebody on this street has her! They can't have gone far! I only left her for a few seconds!'

The woman looks past me and towards the empty pram across the road and only then does she start to share my concern. The look that comes over her face instantly tells me she isn't behind this devious plot because it can only be described as one of pure empathy, mixed in with some horror. She is quickly on my side, asking me if I'm sure about this, asking if I saw or heard anyone, asking if I could be mistaken. But she can see that I'm drowning in a sea of fear, possibly because she has had her own children before so knows this is every parent's worst nightmare. Her kids must be all grown up now and maybe have had little ones of their own. She's potentially a grandmother or maybe even a great grandmother. Whatever she is, she is on my side because she leaves her home and rushes towards me, meeting me as I get halfway up her driveway.

'Have you called the police?' she wants to know, and it's a question that brings this whole crazy time into sharper focus.

The police. Yes, I should call them. Why haven't I done that already? Maybe because doing so is accepting that I've lost all control of this situation and need them to take over from here.

'I haven't,' I say, my voice quiet now, and I'm suddenly overwhelmed with the severity of this situation. Tears begin to roll down my cheeks, and I want nothing more than to collapse onto the ground and pass out, hoping that when I wake up, this will all be over and I'll be reunited with my child.

'I'll phone them,' the woman says, helping me at my time of greatest need or perhaps just recognising that I am completely incapable of making a simple phone call myself. But phone calls do need to be made and not just to the police.

I need to tell Leon about this.

As I see another door opening further down the street and yet one more confused resident appearing, gawking at the distressed woman who has come here and disturbed the peace, I wonder how I'm supposed to tell my husband about what has happened.

About what I've lost.

I know he'll be as devastated as I am; that is a given. But I know something else too. Our child, the one we made together and were raising together, was the only thing keeping us together. We'd never survive as a couple without her. She was our ray of light, our bond, our connection. Our love simply isn't strong enough anymore to have things go back to just the two of us.

I have spent a long time hating Leon for what he did behind my back. But now he has an even bigger reason to hate me. I've lost her. This is my fault.

No one else is to blame but me.

As I hear the kindly woman calling the police, I sink to my knees and wonder what they are going to say to me when they get here. But it's less what they will say and more what they will think.

They'll all be thinking the same thing - the police, these neighbours, and my husband.

Worst of all, I'm thinking it too.

What kind of mother loses their child?

10

I can hear sirens echoing around the city as I put my phone to my ear and wait for Leon to answer my call. The police are clearly on their way, racing towards this part of Stirling, possibly for the first time ever because I doubt anything as serious as this has ever happened on Buckingham Place before.

I know the officers will be here in a moment, joining me and those who are at home this time of day and have come outside to see what is happening. I count seven residents out here now, some of them standing together and talking, presumably about me, while a few stay by themselves in their doorways, watching but not contributing.

'Hello?'

My husband's voice at the other end of the line sounds quiet and weary, and of course it is because he's hungover. Now I'm about to make him feel a whole lot worse.

'Leon! It's me! I need you to listen to me. Something terrible has happened, and I don't know how but it has, and now the police are coming, but we'll get her back, I swear!'

'What? Get who back?'

Unsurprisingly, Leon is totally confused, and he's only going to know what I am talking about if I come out and say the words. But saying them is not simple.

'It's Tuppence,' I start with, hoping my husband can fill in the blanks after that and allow me to not have to go into any more detail.

'What about her?'

I need to say it.

'Gabby, what's happened? Is she okay?'

'I don't know.'

'What do you mean you don't know?'

This is it. The moment I know we will never be able to come back from if Tuppence isn't found.

'Somebody took her,' I tell him, the words almost catching in my throat but coming out just loud enough for Leon to hear.

'What?'

Don't make me say it again.

'I heard something during our walk. Someone was calling out for help, so I tried to help them. I left her for a second. It was only a second. But-'

'What do you mean you left her? Where is she now?'

'I don't know!'

'Gabby, that's our daughter! Where is she?'

'I don't know!'

I'm wailing down the phone, and the kindly woman who called the police for me comes quickly over to try and comfort me, but it's nowhere near enough. I feel like I can't breathe. I feel like I'm having an anxiety attack. *My heart is racing so fast...*

Now the woman has my phone, taking it from me and telling Leon exactly where we are, what the current situation is and what he needs to do next, which is basically get here as quickly as possible so he can help me and the police try and find our child.

She lowers the phone after giving him our location and goes to hand it back to me, so I guess the call is over and Leon is on his way, but the police are going to beat him here. The sirens are louder now, meaning they're closer, and I can see flashes of blue reflecting back off the windows at the end of the street. Then the first car arrives, turning the corner and driving towards us, quickly followed by another one. A third car parks at the end of the row, but the first two only stop when they reach me, and I prepare myself for this to get even more real.

I wish Leon was here, but I also know that he can't answer the questions I'm going to be asked because I was the one who was with Tuppence, so I'm the only one who might have any information that can help find her.

Why did Leon have to be hungover? If he'd been in a more suitable state then he would have been with me on this walk, and one of us could have stayed with the pram. Or why couldn't those woman's cries for help been yesterday or the day before when Leon was pushing the pram around here on his own? I doubt he would have been so bothered as to go and investigate the noise. He probably would have strolled right past, probably not even hearing the cries with his headphones in his ears, his mind elsewhere, totally oblivious, and if that had been the case, Tuppence would have been safe with him.

Why did this have to happen on my watch?

The first police officer is pointed in my direction and when he reaches me, he asks me if I'm the mother. I nod my head before he asks me to talk him through exactly what happened, which I do as quickly as I can because there surely isn't any time for long conversations. We need action, and after giving him a description of Tuppence, including what colour clothes she was wearing, which was a light pink baby sleepsuit beneath a cream coloured coat, I'm hoping I'm going to get it.

'You say you heard the woman's voice from behind that house?' he asks me, looking towards the pram and the property I stupidly went looking around when my sole focus should have been my daughter's safety.

'Yes! But there was no one there! They must have tricked me!' I cry, and quickly, two officers are directed to go and check the house, although I tell them nobody answered the door when I knocked.

More people come out onto the street now that the police cars are here, and while it seems like additional people are helping, it's actually making me feel stressed because the more chaotic this setting becomes, surely the harder it will be to locate the little girl amongst it all.

This is probably what the kidnapper wants and expects, I think. *While all this craziness is occurring, they are getting away with my child.*

'Please, you have to be quick! You have to find her now before it's too late!' I beg the officer as another police car arrives, this one at the other end of the street, and while they're not exactly blocking the road, they have made a cordon of sorts. That's why I hope Tuppence is still on this street somewhere. If she's already beyond the police cars, will we ever get her back?

'Somebody here must know something,' I say defiantly. 'Tuppence must be around here. Somebody knew where we were and what we were doing. We'd been watched, and I was tricked into leaving her. Somebody on this street has her, I just know it. You need to search all these houses! Do it now! Please!'

The officer looks overwhelmed by the orders I'm giving him, or perhaps wondering why I consider myself qualified to make predictions about the outcome of this case. Either way, he doesn't do anything until he sees another car arrive. This one is unmarked and the man who steps out from behind the wheel of it is not wearing a uniform that marks him out as a policeman either. He is wearing a smart suit and his tie jiggles as he paces towards me. He looks like a man of purpose and he sure has one here.

Find my baby.

'Detective Jacobs,' he says as he surveys me and then the scene around us. 'I want to assure you that these police officers are doing everything they can to locate your daughter.'

'But they're not doing everything! They aren't searching these houses. They aren't questioning these residents. Somebody here has done this!'

'Please try and stay calm. If not for me then for your daughter. She needs you right now. It might not seem it but you are her best hope because only you know exactly what happened. So let's talk. Tell me what you know.'

The detective is right, so I rush through the story and once I have, he marches away from me and gives out several sets of instructions to several very willing officers. By the looks of it, he is doing what I asked, or at least partly. He is having some of his officers speak to the residents who are standing around outside their homes, while he is sending others into gardens and even a few off the street and into the surrounding ones.

Darkness has fallen now, so only the streetlights and the headlights from the police cars are offering us any light and that will surely hinder the search, but they can only work with the conditions they have got. I feel some of my strength returning as I watch them because they seem to know what they are doing, and decide that I need to start searching too but just before I can, I hear a familiar voice.

'Gabby?'

I turn around and see Leon sprinting towards me, and he's very much out of breath when he reaches me.

'What's happening?' he wants to know, his eyes wide and reflecting back the flashing blue lights that surround us.

'They're trying to find her,' I tell him, wondering why Leon hasn't tried to comfort me yet or if he ever will.

'I don't understand. How did this happen?' he asks then as he sees the empty pram being looked into by the detective, who then goes down the side of the house I told him about.

'I don't know,' I reply meekly, not having the energy to run through it all one more time, before I quit waiting for my husband to hold me and fall into his arms myself.

I let out a load of tears as his weight supports mine, sobbing into his shoulder and telling him again and again how sorry I am that this has happened. My desperation seems to be the thing that makes him realise just how bleak this situation is, and I sense his body weakening too, his usually strong arms softening as I try to find a little slice of comfort from inside him.

When I lift my head up and look into my husband's eyes, they seem vacant, like he's not really in there. But if that's how he feels, I feel exactly the same way, like neither of us want to be ourselves anymore and we'd give anything to be able to swap our lives with someone else's. Of course we would. It would be better to be anybody else other than a parent who doesn't know where their child is.

As I wipe away my tears and wonder how much Leon must hate me, I see somebody else has joined the fray. A couple of houses down, stood amongst a group of pensive-looking pedestrians and two police officers who are watching on, I see Raquel. She is standing outside her home with her daughter in her arms, and she is looking right at me.

That's when I scream and tell everybody here that she is the person who has taken my baby.

11

'Where is she? I know you have her!' I cry as I rush towards Raquel, my finger pointing in her direction because I want all the police officers here to know exactly who I am talking to.

Raquel looks surprised by my outburst, but as I get closer to her, I can't believe how I didn't realise this before. She lives on this street. She's been watching me. She is grieving for a daughter and saw me with mine.

She saw a way to replace the child she lost.

'It's you, I know it is!' I say as I reach Raquel, but I'm stopped from getting any closer by a police officer who quickly steps in between us, presumably to protect the object of my anger as well as the baby she is holding in her arms. I feel somebody pulling at my arms then and look back to see Leon behind me, trying to slow me down too.

'I've seen you spying on us!' I shout, looking back at Raquel. 'You were outside our accommodation! You wanted Tuppence, didn't you? You want a sister for your child! But she's my daughter, not yours! So where is she?'

Raquel turns away from me, shielding herself and her baby from any more of my vitriol, but I'm not going to give up that easily, and while we're kept apart, I keep shouting, demanding that these officers search her home and question her.

Detective Jacobs is quickly beside me to find out what all the noise is about, so I make sure to tell him about the conversation I had with Raquel in the pub when I first met her and the fact she has been watching us ever since. As Raquel goes inside, the detective tells a couple of officers to go and speak to her and they catch up with her on her doorstep before they start talking, though I can't hear what is being said. I can hear Leon telling me to calm down though.

'You screaming isn't helping anybody,' he says to me, and for the first time since he arrived, I detect disdain dripping from his voice.

He looks angry now, and annoyed, but not at whoever the kidnapper is. *He's angry at me.*

'How the hell did you let this happen?' he asks me as he puts his hands on his head and starts pacing around. 'How did you lose our daughter?'

'It was an accident!' I cry, but I know that's not the truth. 'No, it was planned! Somebody tricked me!'

I'm the victim here.

Aren't I?

Leon isn't looking at me like I am the victim though, nor are a few of the police officers moving around this street, although they might not necessarily be judging me and more just feeling frustrated that a quiet shift tonight has turned into a massive manhunt. It certainly has because a moment later, I hear the sound of a helicopter, and as it begins circling overhead, I know the pilot has joined in the search now too.

We have eyes on the ground and in the sky, so surely that's a good thing.

But what if Tuppence isn't outside where she can be seen?

What if she's already successfully hidden away?

That's when I beg Detective Jacobs to search all the houses in the area again. The helicopter can cover the streets and the gardens, not to mention members of the public who can always report anything suspicious they see. But it's inside these homes where the secrets lie because we don't have eyeballs there and we need to change that fast.

I look back at Raquel, but she is no longer outside her house, having gone in with the two officers who went to speak to her, and I tell myself that if she is guilty then they will surely get her to crack and give herself away. Tuppence is nearby; call it a mother's sense but I just know it, although if she is near, why can't I hear her crying out for her mummy?

I don't want to entertain the thought that somebody has taken her not to keep her for themselves but to hurt her, so I stop thinking like that and watch Detective Jacobs giving out more instructions to his team. Leon is still nearby too, pacing around with his hands still on top of his head, his fingers interlinked, his legs moving fast, his face a grimace, all sure signs of anxiety overriding his body and forcing him to lose control of it.

'I need you to come to the station and answer some more questions,' Detective Jacobs says to us. 'Both of you. We will continue to conduct our search and let you know what we find, but for now, we need you to come and assist this investigation away from here.'

'I'm not leaving until I know where my daughter is,' I reply, terrified of walking away from the last place

I saw my girl. 'Why can't you ask me the questions here?'

'Because there's too much going on, and neither you nor your husband are going to be in the right frame of mind here.'

'I'm not going to be in the right frame of mind anywhere. Not until I get my daughter back!'

'Just listen to the detective, he's trying to help us,' Leon says with great exasperation. 'Stop telling people what to do when you clearly haven't got a clue yourself!'

I stare at Leon, stunned at his outburst, but he doesn't even look at me. He just tells Jacobs that he'll do whatever he needs to do and that only makes me feel like I am hindering things rather than helping. That's why I go along with the plan and follow Jacobs to his car, and as Leon and I get into the back seat beside each other, neither one of us dares say a word to the other.

Leon presumably doesn't speak because he'll say something about me that he might later regret, and I don't speak because I don't want to hear it.

It's a short drive to Stirling police station, and all the way there, I can see the beam from the helicopter that is circling over the city, the bright ray of light piercing through the dark sky and shining down on certain points, illuminating the darker parts of this place. Gardens. Alleyways. Shadowy streets. I'm assuming those in the helicopter have not seen anything of interest yet because they don't seem to be hovering over any fixed point, rather just moving around in a sweeping fashion, looking busy but so far, proving ineffective. I wonder if they'll end up being any help at all or whether it'll be the boots on the ground who make the breakthrough. If there's a breakthrough to be made, that is.

'Stop the car. I'm going to be sick,' I shout out to the driver before reaching for the door handle, and as the car comes to a stop, I have to put my free hand to my mouth. I feel extremely nauseous, and as I open the door and step outside, the burst of fresh air is the only thing that keeps the sickness at bay.

Leaning over with my hands on my knees, I suck in several deep breaths, as if flooding my body with extra oxygen will make up for the fact that Tuppence is missing. But it won't, and I'm aware this hell I am in is only just beginning.

Only getting worse.

I feel a hand on my shoulder then, so I tell Leon that I can't do this. I can't go to the police station. I can't answer questions. I can't do anything because my world is imploding and there's no stopping it now. Then I hear a voice that isn't my husband's and realise he's not the one standing with me at all.

The hand belongs to Detective Jacobs. Leon is still sitting on the backseat of the car and when I see him, he's not even looking at me.

He really does blame me for this.

'We're going to do everything we can to get your daughter back, I promise,' Jacobs tells me, removing his hand because maybe he's thought it's not very professional of him to be touching a witness. Or am I a suspect?

'You know I'm telling you the truth, right?' I ask fearfully. 'Please don't waste time thinking we had anything to do with this because that will only give the kidnapper more of a chance of getting away!'

'Nobody has suggested you or your husband have done anything untoward here,' Jacobs tells me, but he could just be saying that to get me back in the car, and once we're at the station, he'll go from being my best friend to my worst enemy.

I've seen the news, and I've watched the TV shows. I know how this works. The parents of a missing child are always suspects unless somebody else draws the police's attention away.

I can't say I'm feeling any better, but I also know that I can't stand by the roadside much longer, listening to Jacobs tell me to get back in the car, as well as the helicopter's engine churning away overhead. That's why I reluctantly get back into the vehicle, sitting alongside Leon again, and this time he does bother to look at me. He also has something to say and when I hear it, it might not be the wisest thing he could have said in the back of a detective's car.

'Whatever happens and whoever did this, it's our fault, isn't it,' he says, which sounds like more of a statement than a question. 'We wouldn't even be in Stirling if we weren't having problems. We came here because our marriage is messed up. Now we'll end up leaving here without the only good thing that came from our marriage.'

I don't know what to say to that, and those sobering words are left ringing in my ears as we move on in the direction of the police station. All the while, the helicopter keeps going around and around in the sky like the paranoid thoughts inside my head.

12

Leon and I have quite a history and it's that history that is being picked apart by Detective Jacobs now. Having gone over the circumstances of Tuppence's disappearance several times, the conversation, or perhaps I should say interrogation, has moved onto the two people tasked with protecting the missing child.

'Has anything like this ever happened before?' Jacobs enquires, and it's a question that I resent because of what it insinuates.

It's basically him saying *I know your daughter is only young, but have you ever lost her before? If so, well, you really are terrible parents, aren't you?*

'No, never,' Leon snaps back, his patience as tested as mine, and Jacobs nods his head.

'How would you say you've adapted to your new responsibility since Tuppence was born?' he asks then, another loaded question, hinting that we've both struggled with it and that's contributed to us being neglectful and losing her.

'It's been hard, but it's wonderful too,' I say, making it clear that being a mother to my daughter is a dream come true. 'I wouldn't change her for the world. She's gorgeous. She's-'

My emotions get the better of me there, and Leon has to finish my sentence as I pick up one of the tissues Jacobs laid out on the table between us earlier.

'She's great,' my husband confirms. 'We love her, and we'd never do anything to hurt her, so can we stop wasting time and figure out where she is?'

Jacobs is pleasant but clearly has no interest in being told how to lead his investigation, so he pauses briefly before carrying on.

'How has your relationship been since she was born?' he asks us then, and while that's a fair enough question, it comes with a very complicated answer.

Should either of us get into our troubles? The webcam girls? The fact we came to Stirling to try and keep our family together? How I have thought about divorce several times over the past few months? No, I'd rather not get into any of that, not just because it's embarrassing but because it's irrelevant. Leon seems to agree.

'We're fine,' he says, that simple word covering up the reality. 'We're happily married, and we were in this city on holiday. We came here because we presumed it was safe, but even if something unexpected did happen, we presumed the police would help us. So now we need you, why aren't you helping?'

Leon has cleverly turned this back onto the detective and I'm actually proud of him for that because he should be the one under pressure to get results. He has far more resources than we have to locate Tuppence and if she isn't found, he'll be the one who the public are asking questions of, not her poor parents.

'It's funny,' Jacobs says, leaning back in his seat. 'You say you're happily married yet in all the time I've been around you, I haven't once seen any sign of that. You haven't held hands. You spent most of the car journey here avoiding eye contact with one another. You barely spoke. It was me who consoled your wife by the roadside earlier, not you.'

Jacobs has got Leon there, which is probably why my husband has nothing to say in response to that, so I chip in after wiping my eyes once more with my tissue.

'We've had our issues, and we came here to get away from them. But honestly, they have nothing to do with what's happened. Leon was hungover so stayed back at the house, and I was pushing Tuppence in her pram following a route that we have followed for the past three nights. Everything was normal until I heard that woman shouting for help. You have to find that woman. She is the one who did this, or she is part of it, at least.'

Jacobs must have a good radar for honesty because he gives me a nod before altering his line of enquiry.

'Is there anything unusual that has happened during your trip? Anything at all before Tuppence went missing.'

Leon and I share a look, but he doesn't seem to have anything to bring up, though I do.

'I told you about Raquel,' I say. 'How I had an awkward interaction with her in the pub and how I saw her standing outside our accommodation, meaning she might have followed us there.'

'Yes, and my officers have been speaking to her, and we will make a search of her home, as we will all the homes in the vicinity. But is there anything else?'

'What else do you need? I just told you Raquel was acting weird. It can't be a coincidence that this happened only a few doors down from where she lives!'

'If she is involved in any way, we will find out,' Jacobs replies, his tone of voice carrying a weight of experience in solving crimes. 'But is there anything else or anyone else? Anything at all that could help us?'

I rack my brains but there isn't, and that's when I realise I really am pinning my hopes on it being Raquel because if not, I'm as clueless as the police currently are.

'What happens now? Can we go and look for our daughter, or do we have to stay here?' Leon asks, looking utterly drained. He needs sleep, as do I, not a night spent wandering the streets of Stirling looking for our little girl, but that's what we'll be doing. Or at least that's what we hope to be doing if we're allowed out of here.

'We'll need you to stay here until we have conducted a search of your accommodation,' Jacobs says. 'After that, you may leave, but I can't have you on Buckingham Place hampering our investigation,' Jacobs tells me. 'I need you to be contactable because we may have more questions or need to update you on developments. What I cannot have is either of you banging on doors and accusing people. It's our job to investigate. All you can do is support each other during this time.'

'You want to search where we're staying?' I ask. 'Why?'

'Come on, Gabby, it's obvious,' Leon says wearily. 'They have to rule us out as suspects, and no matter how much we tell them they're wasting their time looking into us, they still have to do it.'

Jacobs doesn't disagree with any of what was just said, and I suppose the quickest way for us to get out of here is to let the police do whatever they have to do. But even though we're sat right next to each other, it still feels as if there is a chasm between Leon and me, and once we're out, I'm not sure how much support we will actually be giving each other. But getting Tuppence back is far more important than our squabbles, and I hope my husband thinks that way too.

'One more thing,' Jacobs says. 'The press will be all over this. It'll be obvious there is a big story in the city, and they'll have lots of questions. Please consult with me before you speak to anybody, you understand?'

'Can we use the media to help us?' I ask. 'Do a press conference or something?'

'That's an option available to us, but for the time being, we'll proceed as we are. Hopefully, it won't get that far along that we'll need to do such a thing.'

I'm hoping that too because the thought of going on live television and weeping in front of the nation is an awful one.

Jacobs reiterates how important it is for us to support one another, before he shows us out of the room we've just been talking in, and we're then informed that a liaison officer called David will assist us from here.

The officer, a short, blonde-haired man in his twenties, looks nervous as he approaches us, as if he hasn't had much experience of this before, and maybe he hasn't because how many people go missing around here on a daily basis? It might even be easier for him to deal with families who know what have happened to their loved ones, even if it's bad news, because at least then they have answers. But for Leon and I, there are no answers, only so many questions that this liaison officer is certainly not qualified to answer.

'We want to go out and look for our daughter,' Leon tells David, who understands but tells us we have to remain at the station until the police have carried out some checks into us. That's frustrating, but we tell anyone who will listen that once those checks are complete, we want to be taken as close to the street where Tuppence vanished as possible. We'll begin our search from there, and we'll walk around until dawn, if we have to, in the hope that we'll find something that gives us a clue as to where she is.

I imagine that when we park at the end of Buckingham Place, I will see all the police cars are still there, though all the residents will probably have gone back inside their homes. Of course they will have, it'll be late and cold, and perhaps most crucially, it's not their child that is missing. They will care but only up to a certain point. No one will care as much as the two heartbroken parents staring dumbfounded at the police officers combing the gardens, looking for any sign of our girl or a sign that she might have been harmed during her kidnapping.

They have a grim task, looking for evidence of a crime and hoping to find it so they have something to go on, but what they find might be traumatising. I almost don't know whether I want them to find something or not. Unless they find Tuppence alive and well, is it better to not find anything than to find something bad?

Torn baby clothes.

Blood.

A body.

The search will go on.

But will it ever end?

13

We remained at the police station while a search of our rental accommodation was carried out. But nothing untoward was found, as expected, or at least expected by us anyway, and we were eventually told we could leave. Since then, and following the detective's advice, Leon and I have stayed off Buckingham Place, allowing the police officers to conduct their searches without our interference. But we are being as proactive as we can and have been walking all around Stirling beneath a light drizzle, an image of our baby girl on each of our phones, which we are showing to anybody we pass. Unfortunately, given the late hour, we don't see that many people, though we approach the ones we do and ask them, if not beg them, to look at the photo and see if they can remember seeing this child at some point during the evening.

But so far, no one has.

Some people have glanced at the image on our phones for a mere second before shaking their heads while others have really had a good look at it to be sure about the answer they give. But all the answers have been the same.

"No, I haven't seen her. Sorry."

As I watch Leon go over to a homeless man sitting in the doorway of a closed department store, I look around for my own person to ask next. But the street is deserted - still several hours until sunrise when all the businesses here open for locals and tourists to descend for a morning coffee to help them begin their day.

Leon returns to me, having not had any luck with the homeless man, and when he arrives, he looks even more despondent and down on his luck than the person he just spoke to. That guy has obviously fallen on hard times if he's sleeping on the streets, but I bet Leon would give anything to swap places with him now because anything would be better than being in his shoes or mine.

The drizzle that has been falling from the dark sky overhead has soaked the pair of us, as well as David, our designated family liaison officer who has been with us ever since he was introduced to us, pretending to be helping but also keeping an eye on us. Does he think we'll run? Or maybe Detective Jacobs does? Either way, we wouldn't be being shadowed if they completely trusted us.

However, one good thing about this wet weather is that the water on my face is mixing in with tears, making it less obvious that I've been crying during my time out here. But it also makes it harder for me to tell if Leon has been crying too because droplets of rain are falling from his forehead down into his eyes and as he wipes more of them away, I wonder if there were a few tears in there too.

As we carry on our grim task, wandering around a mostly empty city like lost ghosts whose souls are unable to settle, it becomes more and more obvious to me that there is a question looming that neither of us wants to ask or answer.

At what point do we give up and go home?

I'm sure David can't wait to get indoors, but he knows better than to tell us what to do at a time like this, but maybe we should make the decision for him. I check the time and see that it is after three o'clock in the morning. Realistically, we're not going to see many more people out here until sunrise, so the potential rewards of what we are doing are diminishing rapidly. But yet we persist, neither one of us willing to call it quits because to do so is akin to giving up. However, I am aware we can't wander around out here all night, not just because it's probably futile but because we'll both quickly get ill from this exposure to the damp and cold, if we're not going to be ill already. And then, just after three-thirty, it happens.

'We should go back to the house,' Leon says after we have just walked down yet another empty street. 'We can come out again when the sun's up if the police haven't found anything by then. If we go back, they'll find us quicker too if they need to speak to us.'

'That's a good idea,' David says quickly, predictably keen to get out of the rain and take a seat somewhere dry.

I really don't want to stop searching, but my husband is right. What he says makes sense without him having to also mention the fact that if we do stay out here all night, we're going to be even more exhausted than we otherwise would be if we were sat in our rented accommodation. We'll still be bereft as we sit on the sofa and stare at the four walls, but at least we'll be warm and dry. But is Tuppence warm and dry herself, or is she out here somewhere, exposed to these elements? I pray that she isn't and, wherever she is, that she is at least comfortable. But who knows?

It's gone four o'clock by the time we make it back to the house, and as we walk through the door, I check my phone again on the off chance that I have somehow missed a call from Detective Jacobs, who has been trying to ring me with good news. But I haven't, though I already knew that because my ringer is on full volume, as is Leon's, so any phone calls to us with an update would have been heard loud and clear out on silent streets.

'I'll put the kettle on,' David says after we have gone inside and taken off our wet coats in the hallway, and I just stare at him helplessly as he goes to do such an arbitrary thing as make us both a cup of tea.

As I hear the kettle boil, I dread going into another room because I know this hallway is the only room in here that doesn't contain any of Tuppence's things. If I go into the lounge, I will see her changing mat and toys. If I go in the kitchen, I will see her bottles and milk. If I go in the bathroom, I will see her yellow rubber ducky in the tub. And if I go into the bedroom, I will see her crib standing next to our bed, and the sight of that will almost certainly have me on my knees and begging for a positive outcome. Leon seems reluctant to make a move too, so neither of us do.

We stay in the hallway until David appears again, emerging from the kitchen with two cups in his hands, and he seems surprised to find us exactly where he left us a few minutes ago. But he soon understands why we have been lurking in the hallway rather than going to sit on the sofa when he enters the living area and is met with the sight of all of Tuppence's belongings scattered across the floor.

He stands and stares at her toys, as well as the bag of nappies beside her changing mat, and I know he's regretting walking in and seeing all that. But I know we can't just stand in the hallway all night, so Leon and I reluctantly join him, and I make my way to the sofa whilst trying to keep my eyes from any reminders of our girl. As I sit down, David hands me my drink, and the warmth from the liquid inside the cup provides some comfort. A short sip of tea makes me feel a tiny bit better as well, but things like that are fleeting. I still feel awful, and I know the only reason I'm not crying now is because I've exhausted myself crying for most of the evening.

'We're supposed to check out tomorrow,' Leon says from where he stands by a window, his own cup of tea in hand. That's a grim reminder that despite the chaos currently gripping our lives, there is a rule we must abide by in terms of our stay here and that is that we are supposed to tidy up and leave here by 10 a.m. But how can either of us go about the process of packing when we are so worried about our daughter? If everything was as it should be, all three of us would have left here in the morning and made it to the station in time to board the 10:45 train back to Edinburgh. But we won't be on that train. We'll still be in Stirling, or at least Leon and I will be. God knows where Tuppence is now, but until we get some clue that suggests she is elsewhere, we will stay here and keep searching. I don't know where we'll stay while we remain here looking, but we'll figure it out. I'll sleep on the streets if I have to. Whatever happens, I'm not leaving here tomorrow without my baby.

'Try not to worry about that just yet,' David says. 'We can make sure you have somewhere to stay.'

That's helpful, I suppose, but David's presence here is just another reminder of how abnormal this situation is. I can tell that Leon hates having him around too because he's barely said a word to him all night, but David seems used to this kind of treatment.

'You should both try and get some sleep,' he says after we have finished our drinks, the pair of us having sipped in silence until our cups are empty. 'I'll stay up in case anyone from the police tries to get in touch. But you two should try and rest.'

'I can't sleep,' I reply quickly, almost irritated that he would even suggest that I could.

'You should try,' Leon chips in then. 'I can stay up. I can function after an all-nighter, I've done it enough times when I've been out with friends, but you can't. You need your sleep, even if it's just a couple of hours.'

'It's not a choice I'm making,' I say to Leon, growing even more frustrated, 'I physically can't sleep, and I know I won't be able to until she's back, so stop telling me what to do.'

Leon wisely doesn't challenge me on that, nor does David, so we return to silence, allowing more time to pass by during which none of us can do anything more meaningful than wish for some good news when the sun rises.

Leon and I know we are in limbo and our fates will be decided by only one thing now.

Whether or not our daughter is returned to us alive.

14

I open my eyes to see the living room bathed in sunlight and as I look around, I realise that despite my firm belief, I was able to achieve sleep at some point. The last thing I remember is me sitting here in the dark looking at photos of Tuppence on my phone, which was tormenting, but I did it anyway. But my eyelids had been growing extremely heavy, and I guess fatigue overwhelmed me eventually and I was blessed with a brief respite from the hell of consciousness. But I'm awake again now and back in a world of pain.

The churning sensation I feel in my stomach is awful, just like the pressure headache I have from feeling so stressed. *Please let there be some good news today*, I think. *Please let this be the day that Tuppence is returned to us.*

But currently, the only thing that I know for certain will happen today is that Leon and I are due to check out of our accommodation. This is our departure day, though we're obviously not in any fit state to check out. I haven't packed a thing, though when I go into the bedroom to find Leon, I discover him with our luggage on the bed, suggesting he's in a productive mode.

'What are you doing?' I ask him as I watch him putting his clothes into his backpack.

'What does it look like?'

'But we can't leave.'

'We have to check out today.'

'And do what? Go back to Edinburgh and pretend like nothing happened here?'

'I'm not saying that. But we have to leave here, unless you want to book another night?'

'I don't know what I want to do yet, but we can't leave without Tuppence.'

'Do you think I want to do that? I'm not the one who lost our child.'

Leon looks like he instantly regrets the words that just left his mouth, but it's too late to take them back, and I leave the bedroom with tears running down my cheeks, ignoring his pleas to stop and accept his apology. David emerges from the kitchen then and asks me if I'd like another cup of tea, but I just walk past him on my way to the door.

I just want to get out of here now and get some fresh air, and as I head for the front door, I'm hoping I can get outside before anyone catches up to me. I do, but as I pull the door open, I find a woman on the doorstep.

'Hi. I'm sorry, I didn't mean to disturb you,' she says, and as I take in her red hair and friendly smile, I find her familiar.

'I'm the owner of this property,' she says, and that's where I know her from. I saw her photo online when I booked this place, and if I remember right, her name is Kelly. But why is she here?

'We haven't packed yet,' I say, afraid that we're now about to be rushed out of this house, and being rushed is the last thing I need at the moment.

'Oh, don't worry. I don't expect you to,' Kelly says, surprising me. 'I just wanted to let you know that you can stay for as long as you like.'

I'm confused, but Kelly soon explains.

'The police were in touch with me regarding searching my property,' Kelly says. 'I gave them permission to conduct that search, but only after I had asked to know what was happening. I'm so sorry about your daughter. I'm sure she will be found soon.'

Kelly's sympathy is sweet but what she says next is not.

'I also came to check on you guys because there's been a lot of things posted on social media.'

'Social media?'

'Yes, there were photos online and news about what's happened. I just want you to know that you don't have to leave yet. You can stay here as long as you need. I can cancel the next booking after you. Just focus on finding your daughter.'

What this woman is saying to me is very kind, but it's also disconcerting. There are photos of me on social media? What photos? And what are people saying about me? Are the trolls and keyboard warriors already calling me the world's worst mother?

'Sorry, what's on social media?' I ask. 'Can you show me?'

'Oh, of course,' Kelly replies before taking out her phone and doing a bit of scrolling. But before she can get any further, David arrives behind me, and he says that me seeing what's online might not be the best thing. He then offers to talk me through what is going on back inside the house, but I ignore him, as I've already started to do, and tell Kelly to show me what she is referring to.

When she holds up her device and I take a look, I see an image of me on my knees and it must have been taken on Buckingham Place when that neighbour was calling the police for me. But who took the photo? It must have been one of the other neighbours, a witness to the drama that had begun unfolding on the usually silent part of suburbia. Then they posted it online for everybody to gawk at, as if my privacy isn't important enough. But then again, what is private about any of this? The police cars. The helicopter. The speculation from everybody living in this city as to what is going on. It's only a matter of time until this becomes huge news, broadcast on all the big media channels in Scotland and maybe around the rest of the UK too, if it hasn't happened already. Then I really can kiss goodbye to any last vestige of privacy I might want.

Everybody will know what's happened.

Everybody will know what I've lost.

'What's going on?' Leon asks as he arrives in the doorway behind me and David, and Kelly quickly lets him know why she is here, before asking if there is anything she can do to help us. There isn't, beyond what she has already kindly offered, so I thank her, before telling her that I need to go and speak to the police, and she understands and leaves us alone.

'Forget the packing. We don't have to leave,' I tell Leon as I prepare to be on my way again, but he grabs my arm before I can walk away from the house.

'Wait a minute. We need to talk about this. About what we do if there's no news today. Or tomorrow. We can't just stay here forever looking for her. We have our jobs in Edinburgh.'

'Who cares about our jobs?' I cry. 'Our only goal is to find Tuppence.'

'What if we can't find her? What if we never see her again?'

I don't know if Leon's dreadful negativity is a result of him having a sleepless night or if it is just him trying to be practical but either way, it's not appreciated.

'We will find her!' I tell him, insistent to the point of delusion, but how else can I be? Then I try to pull away from him, eager to release myself from his grip, but he keeps hold of me as David watches on. Then my husband says something very honest.

'Don't you get it? Whoever has her is clever, and we have to be prepared that this is it. We might never get her back!'

That's a brutal assessment of the situation, and David tries telling us not to jump to such conclusions, but perhaps Leon is simply trying to provide some balance here because we can't both be positive, can we? Somebody has to be realistic. The problem is, I can't be around realism, so I decide to make that clear.

'If you want to give up on our daughter, fine,' I say to Leon as David winces slightly behind him. 'Go ahead and go back to Edinburgh. Tell everybody how your wife lost your child. How it was all my fault, and it was a waste of time even trying to find her again. But I'm not giving up. I'm not leaving this city until we have her, and I don't care if I have to stay here for years. I'm not giving up!'

I storm away from the house then, desperate to be rid of Leon and David. Feeling unable to count on the support of my partner, I wonder if it might actually be better if he does return to Edinburgh and leave me here to look by myself. But will he actually do that? Surely he'll stay. This family is already broken up enough. But feeling like I can't count on him anymore, which may also be how he feels about me, given what I've lost, I need to call somebody who will always be on my side, and ignoring David's calls for me to come back, I take out my phone from my pocket.

Dreading the exchange I'm about to have with my mother, because I know how much she adores her granddaughter, I call her and brace myself to turn her world upside down. Sharron, my mum and the woman who raised me so well, does not deserve the bad news that she is about to hear. But it's time I told her, not just because she'll most likely hear on the news soon anyway but because she should hear it from me and once she does, I know she'll be racing towards Stirling to join me and the search for Tuppence. Too bad if Leon doesn't want to be a part of that search, but whatever.

Maybe I don't need him. I'm the one who caused this whole mess so maybe I can fix it on my own. What if I'm able to help the police get Tuppence back? I'd be redeemed, right? Nobody could blame me then because I'd have fixed the problem.

That's what I'm going to do.

I'm going to get my daughter back.

But first, I need to tell my mum why her granddaughter won't be home today.

15

It's now twenty-four hours since Tuppence went missing and while a lot has happened in that time, the only thing I wanted to happen has not. There is still no sign of my little girl, no breakthrough from the police, no arrests, no progress, no good news. What there has been is a lot of noise, distraction and stress.

As I expected, no sooner had I told my mum what happened, she had got into her car and driven to Stirling to be with me. Having her by my side has been a big help, certainly far more of a help than having Leon or David there because neither of them are offering much for me, for differing reasons. Leon is still blaming me for what happened and is becoming increasingly withdrawn, whilst David continues to shadow me but has little to offer barring a suggestion to make yet another cup of tea. Thankfully, Mum is more use and as well as giving me several hugs, she has given Detective Jacobs and a few of his colleagues a firm talking to so that they are under no illusions about the task ahead of them.

'Find my granddaughter,' Mum has said to every member of law enforcement that she has come across since arriving in Stirling, and she's seen a lot because she's been with me, walking the streets and lurking around Buckingham Place, desperately seeking updates. It was just before midday when Detective Jacobs confirmed that all the homes on Buckingham Place had been searched and nothing untoward had been discovered, which seemingly dispelled my theory that my daughter is still on that street somewhere. It was shortly after that when the detective requested that Leon and I hand our phones over so they could be examined, a request that prompted great anger from the pair of us because it again felt like we were being treated as suspects rather than victims. But we eventually did so, if only to not waste any more time, and while our devices have not been returned to us yet, there's nothing on there that will be of any interest to the police, or at least I hope there won't.

They'll be checking our messages, emails and internet searches for anything that might relate to getting away with hiding or harming a child and while there is no such thing on my phone or Leon's, there are several messages between the two of us in which it is obvious we were having problems.

How do I feel about some police officer reading my private messages, messages in which very personal parts of my marriage were discussed? There are things on there that refer to what Leon did with his webcam girls, as well as many messages in which he asks me for forgiveness and I tell him I'm not sure if I can give it. What will Detective Jacobs think when he hears about that? Will it add fuel to whatever theory he has that Leon and I are a couple with something to hide, two people who blamed their child for their problems and got rid of her before pretending to be innocent and hoping to get away with murder?

As if that isn't enough to worry about, Detective Jacobs has told us, via David and his intermediary skills, that a public appeal is being planned, and we will be asked to go in front of the cameras and speak to the media to ask for help in finding our daughter. Despite my initial qualms, I'm far too desperate to get Tuppence back to be worried about stage fright and appearing on live television now and am much more worried that such a development means the police clearly are struggling to get anywhere. Surely a public appeal is a last resort, due to a lack of progress elsewhere. I know detectives like to think that such appeals might spark a memory in a witness or spook the culprit into making a mistake, but does that really happen? Or are public appeals as they seem whenever I've seen them on TV myself, in that it just looks like a lot of desperate and clueless people begging for help from total strangers who, unfortunately, cannot provide that help? Either way, I'll find out tomorrow morning at ten o'clock because that's when I'm due to take a seat beside Leon and Detective Jacobs and address the viewing public.

Before then, another awfully long night awaits me, and I'll need Mum's help to get through it. She held me as the twenty-hour anniversary of Tuppence's disappearing passed, the pair of us conducting a very sombre moment's silence before I completely collapsed and began crying. Leon stood by and watched before going back to our accommodation and pretending to keep busy there. I know he was pretending because Mum and I joined him shortly afterwards and he wasn't doing much, just rummaging in his bag and picking up an empty cup before putting it back down again. He's in limbo; we all are, and there's no end in sight.

**

'You don't have to do this,' Mum says to me as I try not to rub my bleary eyes, the same eyes that a make-up artist offered to brighten up for me earlier, though I refused because I don't want anybody watching to think that I give a damn about my appearance at a time like this.

'If it can help then yes, I do,' I reply, before giving Mum a hug and then looking to Detective Jacobs, who looks like he's ready to go. That's more than can be said for the person standing just behind him. That would be Leon and he looks nervous, though for good reason. As soon as we step through the door to our right, we will walk out in front of a room full of journalists with their pens poised and their cameras pointed. Then we'll sit down in front of a microphone and read our prepared statements. After that, we will face some questions. Then, mercifully, the public appeal will be over and we'll retreat from view, where we will wait and hope for some news to filter in that means all of this was actually worth it.

'Okay, we're ready,' Jacobs says to me and Leon before heading for the door, and Leon follows him. But I linger back for a moment, forcing Mum to ask me what's wrong.

'I'm just wondering if Tuppence is going to see this,' I say. 'Wherever she is being held. There might be a TV on. Her kidnapper might be watching and if he is, Tuppence might see my face on screen. I wonder if she'll recognise me.'

'She'll always recognise you, and she'll see you in person soon enough,' Mum says, trying to stay positive for both of our sakes. Leon has already gone through the door now and is presumably already on television, but there will be an empty seat next to him unless I follow suit, so I take a deep breath and force myself out into the glare of the media for my daughter's sake.

As I expected, it's overwhelming to have so many people looking at me, but I try to heed the advice Jacobs gave me earlier in which he told me not to make eye contact with too many people and look down at the desk in front of me if I start feeling too anxious. However, that's easier said than done and as I take my seat beside Leon, I can see he is fidgeting beneath the table. Thankfully, the detective is far more composed than we are and gets proceedings underway, giving all the journalists here what they came for.

'Tuppence Hartley was last seen outside 17 Buckingham Place, Stirling, at five-twenty-two pm on Wednesday, 6th February,' Jacobs says, not reading from the piece of paper in front of him, which tells me he has already committed the details of this case to memory. 'It has now been thirty-six hours since her disappearance, and despite extensive searching in the Stirling area, my colleagues are yet to locate the missing child, which is why we are now appealing for help from members of the public.'

I can't help but wonder just how many people are tuned in right now. It's a weekday morning, so a lot of people will be at work, but footage from this appeal will be shown across several news bulletins, so it will reach a large audience, not just in Scotland but around the whole of the UK. It will probably end up on YouTube too, meaning people from all around the world could see this. I'm not sure if Tuppence has been taken that far away, but I suppose the more people that know about her, the better.

As an image of my baby girl is projected onto a large screen, and Jacobs runs through a description of what she was wearing on the night she went missing, I notice that Leon is looking down at the piece of paper in front of him. On it are the words he has prepared for this appeal, just like I have my own words on the paper in front of me. Jacobs asked each of us to write a short statement that we would want the kidnapper to hear, something that might make them reconsider their actions and return our daughter to us before it's too late. I did as I was asked, fighting back tears as I wrote, and I expect I'll be fighting back tears when I read it out shortly too. But it's Leon to go first and as Jacobs hands over to him, I glance at my husband as he picks up his statement and starts to read it with shaking hands.

'All we want is our little girl back,' he begins, his voice cracking slightly as he speaks. 'Tuppence belongs at home with her mummy and daddy, and if she is returned, we will forgive whoever has taken her. We just want to know she is safe. Please don't hurt her. Just do the right thing and let this be over.'

Leon stops speaking then and I realise he has finished. His statement was much shorter than the one I have written, but as I see the tears in his eyes, I recognise that it was a monumental achievement just for him to say what he did. Now it's my turn, and I'm almost regretting writing so much, because how am I meant to get through this with so much attention on me?

Briefly looking up from my statement, I see the rows of journalists sitting before me, some with tape recorders, others with laptops and even a few with a notepad and pen. Behind them are the cameras and as the silence grows, I'm aware they're all waiting for me to fill it.

Clearing my throat, I look back at my words and begin reading.

'Many women dream of becoming a mother, and I was no different,' I say, refusing to let the tears that are welling in my eyes stop me from getting through this. 'I didn't care whether I had a boy or a girl. I just wanted a healthy, happy baby. I got one on the day Tuppence was born, and it was love at first sight.'

I wipe my eyes then before continuing.

'She is the perfect little girl,' I say, having made sure I used present tense and not past. 'She is so smiley. Happy. A content child. But she needs me as much as I need her, and we can't be apart any longer. I don't know why you took my daughter, whoever you are, but I do know that you can bring her back. That's all I ask of you. Bring her back. Drop her off at a police station or a hospital or a church or anywhere that she can be taken care of. Run away then hide. I won't look for you. I only want to be back with my baby again.'

My tears are getting harder to contain, but I have one more thing to say, though it isn't written down on the piece of paper. That's because our statements were vetted by the police, and I knew they'd make me remove this if they saw what I wanted to say. But they'll get to hear it now, as will everybody else listening.

'My daughter was last seen on Buckingham Place, and I believe somebody on that street is responsible for her abduction,' I go on as the detective's head turns towards me as he realises I'm going off-script. 'Somebody there organised this and somebody there knows what happened. Somebody must have seen. Somebody is hiding something. Somebody on that street has a secret. So if you live on that street and you are watching this now, I want you to know that I will find out what happened, and I will get my daughter back.'

That's all I'm able to say before I realise that my microphone has stopped working and as Jacobs begins speaking into his, concluding the appeal without the opportunity for questions because I've clearly ruined that, I notice Leon looking at me.

'What are you doing?' he asks me, clearly confused, but I don't care what he or anyone else thinks. A mother's intuition is rarely wrong and that's why I said what I did.

Buckingham Place holds the key to getting Tuppence back.

Now that street has everybody's attention.

16

I don't regret telling the media and the public that I believe someone on that street has my daughter, or at least knows who has her, which is why I'm not sorry for the fact that so many people are speculating online about the residents who live there.

And there is a lot of speculation online.

I know that because I have been using Mum's phone to check various social media sites after the public appeal, and that's how I've seen all the comments that are being made after what I said about Buckingham Place.

"It's always the rich who have something to hide."

"I've seen those houses on the news, and they look creepy. Something about that level of affluence just makes me feel icky."

"I think the mother is right. Somebody on that street knows something."

"You know what I always say - big homes house big secrets."

There are hundreds more comments just like that on the internet and more are being added every minute, and frankly, while I wanted to draw attention to that street, I wasn't quite expecting this. But what I did expect was that Detective Jacobs would be annoyed at me for deviating from my prepared statement, and annoyed he is.

'You shouldn't have said that,' he told me shortly after we had left the room full of journalists. 'There is no evidence to suggest any of those residents have done anything wrong, and now you've put them at the centre of this case, which I'm going to get the blame for.'

But I just brushed off the detective's concerns by reiterating my firm belief that Buckingham Place holds the key to solving this whole mystery.

Jacobs stormed off after that, as did Leon, leaving me and Mum to check the damage online, and after seeing all the comments, I shrugged and figured that if I was right, I'd surely just made things harder for the kidnapper. With Buckingham Place at the forefront of this, nobody living there is going to have an easy time of things over the next few days and that's perfect if any one of them has something to hide. But while dealing with the detective was easy enough, it's harder to deal with Leon, and by the time Mum and I go back to the townhouse, I see that, after I surprised him during the appeal, he is now taking his turn to surprise me.

'I'm going home,' he says, and he has the packed bag beside him to prove it.

'What? You can't go home. We have to stay here!' I cry, shocked at his plan.

'And do what? Sit around and hope something happens? Because so far, nothing has happened and anything that we can do here can be done at home. It's up to the police now. We've made our appeal, and there's nothing else we can do.'

'That's not true,' I tell Leon, but I'm not sure it's really the case. Barring another stint walking around Stirling asking if anybody has seen my daughter, I don't know what else we have to offer. But that doesn't mean we just pack up and leave, does it?

'Mum. Tell him! He can't leave!' I cry, hoping my mother will back me up here. But she doesn't say what I was hoping she would.

'Each of you needs to do what you feel is best,' she says. 'If you want to go home, Leon, then you should go home.'

'But we should be together!' I try, and that's when I see that the main reason Leon wants to go is because he knows that I will stay. As he picks up his bag and heads for the door, I sense he wants to get away from me more than he wants to get away from Stirling. But I'm not going to make it easy for him.

'If you walk out that door, that's it! We're finished! Do you hear me?' I shout after him. 'You're abandoning me and Tuppence by leaving. Is that the kind of man you are?'

Mum pleads with me to calm down, but I don't, and I hurl an insult at Leon, but it makes no difference. He doesn't even look back as he walks out of the house and as the door closes behind him, I drop down onto the sofa, and Mum has to hold me again as I cry.

'How can he just leave?' I ask between sobs.

Mum says nothing until I have stopped crying, which is several minutes later, and after she has brought me some tissues, she has a harsh reality check for me.

'It's still early and I'm sure we'll find her,' Mum says. 'But, and I'm not saying this will definitely happen, there may come a time when you do have to leave here and go home. Perhaps Leon is already aware of that and is going now because he thinks it'll be easier than leaving in a few days. He's hurting too, I can see it on his face, and this is his way of coping.'

'By running away?' I cry. 'That's not coping, that's giving up!'

With Leon gone, it feels like this is the end for us, and I react to that realisation by getting up off the sofa and ignoring Mum's pleas for calm as I pick up a lamp and go to hurl it against the nearest wall.

Mum doesn't reach me in time to stop me throwing it and as the lamp shatters on impact, I am already looking for something else to throw. I manage to pull a couple of books off the bookshelf and launch them at the television before Mum grabs hold of my arms and prevents me from breaking anything else in this home that neither of us own. But her holding me is not helping me get out my frustration, so I resort to screaming, a sound that must be horrifying for my mother to hear, as well as shocking for the neighbours to hear too. But with my world ending, what else is there to do?

By the time I calm down again, I am left reflecting on the state of my family, a family that is now as broken as that lamp on the floor. Both Tuppence and Leon are gone, and I don't know what to do next. My heart says I should stay here and pray for news on my daughter, but my head says what Leon's must have already told him, which is that she is gone for good and isn't coming back so it's time to get on with life.

'Help me,' I tell my mum, my voice barely a whisper, and as she holds me, I pray she has a plan. Whatever she says to do next, I will follow because I'm totally lost by myself and am no longer capable of functioning alone.

'I think we should pack up and leave here,' Mum says a moment later. 'We don't have to leave Stirling. We can stay in a hotel. But a change of scene might do you good.'

I'm too tired to argue with that, and after Mum has told me to go and have a lie down while she starts packing, I trudge out of the room. But just before I leave, I pause and look down at the bee toy by my feet. It's the same toy Tuppence was playing with on the morning she went missing, while Leon was in bed with a hangover and I was on my phone looking at property prices on Buckingham Place. As I bend down and pick up the toy, I easily regret spending what was some of my last day with Tuppence staring at my mobile phone screen rather than focusing on her. I should have been more present and savoured every second with my child, rather than take her for granted. But how was I to know that she would soon be snatched?

The soft toy in my hands is providing far less comfort to me than it used to provide for my daughter, and as I turn back and watch my mum putting more of Tuppence's toys into a bag, I wonder if she will ever get to play with any of these again. Or any of the ones back at our house because there are plenty more there.

Leon is going home, but how can he face going into our daughter's bedroom when she's not there? The thought of that is enough to make me feel like I'd rather stay in a hotel for the rest of my life than experience the same thing, but that's not realistic. I'll stay here for a few more days, but, inevitably, if nothing else happens, I'll have to follow Leon home.

I'll have to leave Stirling.

I'll disappear from here just like my daughter did.

17

I arrived in this city by train, but I am leaving it in the passenger seat of my mum's car. It's been five days now since Tuppence was taken, and I think it's time to go home, if only for a short while. I'll be back to Stirling many times, and I'll keep coming back until my daughter is found, but I can't stay here forever, living in limbo and, potentially, getting in the way of the police and their investigation.

Detective Jacobs has no issue with me returning to Edinburgh, and David, the liaison officer, thinks it might help my mental health to have a break from here, though he has promised to check in with me regularly. I didn't have the heart to tell him that such checks will probably make my mental health worse.

Nothing has come from the public appeal we made, besides a few people calling the helpline and offering their theories, none of which have any evidence behind them and all of which have amounted to absolutely nothing. I'm told that it's still early days and I should be hopeful, but I'm also told, mainly by social media comments, that the chances of finding a missing child after this long are not good. I really should stay off the internet because it's full of doom and gloom at the best of times, but it's hard when the whole of Scotland seems to be talking about me online. Some say I'm a bad mother, some say I did nothing wrong, while others seem to enjoy the mystery of it all and just hope they will one day get to find out what really happened.

'Try and get some sleep if you want to,' Mum says as she drives us out of Stirling. 'Don't worry about making conversation. You know me, I'm better off concentrating on the roads than chatting.'

I do know Mum and she is right about that. She must have bumped her car at least three times that I can remember and every one of those times, she put it down to the fact that she was deep in conversation with her passenger and lost focus on the road ahead. We can laugh about it, or at least we used to, because the accidents weren't serious and nobody ever got hurt. But I'd quite like to avoid any incidents today, so I decide to try and take Mum's advice and get some shut-eye before we get home.

Just before I close my eyes, I catch a glimpse of Stirling Castle shrinking in size in the distance, and I think about the day I walked up that hill with Leon and Tuppence. Her in her pram, Leon perspiring from the exertion of pushing her, me ready with my phone to take photos of the view from the top. A simple family memory. It turned out to be one of our last.

Leon and I haven't spoken since he left Stirling ahead of me. The sum total of our communication in the time since has been limited to text messages and even those have been sparse. When we have reached out to one another, it's been about something practical, like Leon looking for something he can't find at the house or me updating him on something Detective Jacobs has told me. There's been no personal communication, no expressions of love, no kisses at the end of messages, not even a simple 'how are you feeling?' or 'did you get any sleep last night?' But neither of us needed this brief break from each other to realise that we're finished, and I assume that once I arrive home, it won't take long for us to make it official.

I'm not sure how the logistics of our separation will work. Hopefully, I can stay at the house and Leon will live elsewhere while we sort out things like the finances. I also hope my husband will be civil with me, because I'll try to be the same with him, and that way, our impending divorce should happen much quicker.

I guess we'll both list 'irreconcilable differences' as our reason for the breakdown of our marriage because isn't that what everyone puts? Those two words can cover all sorts of sins. In our case, they cover webcam girls, a general lack of love and respect and, most of all, they cover up for the fact that Leon blames me for losing Tuppence, while I blame him for being too hungover to be with me that night, which would have made the kidnapper's job much harder if he had been there.

It might have been the rumbling of the car over the tarmac roads or the vibrations from its movement, or maybe it's just because I've barely slept in days, but I do fall asleep, and when I wake, we're approaching Edinburgh. As Mum senses me stirring, she asks me if I'm warm enough, reaching for the switch on the dashboard that controls the heating in here, but I say I'm fine as I rub my eyes. I'm not sure that power nap has done me much good in the grand scheme of things, but it did at least save me from being awake and having to pretend like I'm not utterly depressed around Mum, who

I am conscious of worrying even more than she already is.

As I stare at all the familiar streets that pass by on the other side of my window, my heart aches for the memories I thought I would make here as Tuppence grew. The summers spent mostly at the park. The Christmas markets and lots of treats. The shopping trips. The meals out. The school runs. The swimming lessons. The playdates. The times I would wave her off as a teenager as she went to the cinema or a bar or headed to the Fringe Festival with all the crowds each August. They were all things that were supposed to happen in both of our futures, but now, I don't even know what the future looks like.

I know what my house looks like, of course, and when I see it up ahead, my stomach churns, which is another sure sign that I should separate from Leon. I'm dreading seeing him, and I'm sure the feeling is mutual.

'Do you want me to come inside with you?' Mum asks after she has parked and turned off the engine.

'Maybe just wait here in the car,' I suggest. 'In case it all kicks off.'

I'm hoping we won't argue but just in case, Mum is happy to do as I ask and wait here for me.

I get out of the car and grab my bag, as well as Tuppence's backpack full of things that she used to need on a daily basis, and then slowly head towards the front door. I know Leon is home because his car is parked just in front of Mum's, but I have my key with me anyway, so I won't knock, if only to buy myself a few more seconds of not having to deal with this awful situation.

Letting myself in, I am met by the sight of two suitcases by the door and then Leon coming down the stairs carrying a third. I guess I have my answer about which one of us is going to move out.

'Hey,' he says, stopping on the third step from the bottom when he sees me walking in.

'Hey,' I reply meekly before closing the door, catching a glimpse of Mum sitting behind her steering wheel and feeling glad that she isn't going to hear whatever awkward conversation that is about to occur in this house.

'I'm going to go and stay with Kieran for a few weeks,' Leon says as he finishes coming down the stairs and drops another suitcase by the door. 'He's got the space and he said it's fine. Is that alright?'

'Yeah, fine,' I mutter, thinking briefly about Leon's best friend, Kieran, who got divorced last year, hence why he has all the space. Two male divorcees living together – that sounds pretty grim to me, but for them, maybe it will be one big bachelor party.

'I'm guessing there isn't any news?' Leon asks me, and I shake my head sadly.

'We just have to keep hoping,' he adds then, and I wonder if that's really all we can do.

'I'll go back to Stirling as often as I can,' I say, not wanting Leon to think that I've given up totally on the idea of finding Tuppence.

'Of course,' he says with a sorry nod of the head.

A silence falls between us, and it's pretty pathetic that after all we have been through, from falling in love, getting married and having a baby, we seem to have absolutely nothing to say to each other now.

'I don't know what to do,' I admit.

'Me neither,' Leon replies honestly.

That's enough said to confirm that no amount of counselling, liaison officer meetings, conversations, hugs, prayers and whatever else we could try is going to make any of this better.

It's not just our daughter that has gone.

Our love has vanished too.

By the time Leon has loaded his luggage into his car and Mum has gotten out of hers and come into the house, I am lying on the sofa, tears running down my cheeks and a grim acceptance washing over me that my family has gone for good.

These next few weeks and months are going to be a hell that I have to endure.

The only way I'll get through it is by believing I'll get answers about my girl one day.

For now, even though Mum is still here with me, I just feel totally alone.

18

I mark the one-month anniversary of Tuppence's disappearance by getting blackout drunk in a bar in Edinburgh and requiring the assistance of two strangers to help get me home safely.

The strangers in question are two women in their forties who gently wake me up after I have fallen asleep in a corner booth of a very noisy and very grotty venue. They ask me if I am okay before telling me that they pretended to be my friend to one of the security employees who is preparing to chuck me out onto the streets if I don't wake up and leave of my own accord. I'm far too inebriated to say anything, but I am just about able to haul myself off my makeshift bed and receive the assistance of the two women to get me to the door, and we pass the security guard on the way out - a shaven-headed man in a black uniform who just frowns at me as I leave.

Once outside, the two women help me into a taxi and sit with me on the backseat all the way home, which seems very kind of them, although I soon find out why they have both gone above and beyond to help me tonight. It's as I am stumbling out of the taxi outside my house, and they are helping me find my front door keys in my handbag, when they let slip that they know who I am. They recognise me as the woman in the news, the poor woman who lost her baby in Stirling, and that's why they understand why I have managed to get myself into such a desperate state. They have taken pity on me, mothers themselves who can only imagine the torment I am going through, and like two guardians watching over me tonight, they have ensured I make it back to my home safely.

I want to thank them for their kindness once my front door is unlocked and I am about to step inside, but as I turn my head to look at them, I'm overcome by nausea and end up regurgitating all the drinks I consumed back at that bar. I can't even remember what I was drinking, just that I had a lot, and as the two women grimace and narrowly avoid the puke, I can only wipe my mouth with one of my hands while the other helps keep me balanced in the doorway.

'Are you sure you're going to be okay?' one of the women asks me, but I just wave a dismissive hand at her as if she's asked a stupid question, before tottering backwards a few steps in my high heels and then closing the door. Alone again, I make my way into the kitchen, which takes a while because I keep bumping into the hallway wall as I go. I eventually make it to the fridge and open it in the hopes that there is some white wine inside. But there isn't - I must have finished it before I went out. Or maybe it was last night. I can't remember now. Either way, the house is dry, and my night of binge drinking is over.

Not interested in water or teabags, mainly because neither of those have ever been known for dulling pain like mine, I stagger into my lounge and collapse onto one of the sofas, my handbag falling off my shoulder and the contents spilling out onto the carpet. I wouldn't normally be bothered about picking any of my things up, happy to leave them there on the floor until the morning when I wake up dehydrated and in desperate need of headache tablets. But when I see my phone amongst the discarded items, I swipe for it and just about manage to pick it up without tumbling off the sofa and once I have it, I find the thing I've fallen asleep to for the last several nights.

It's a podcast about Tuppence, or rather the mystery of what might have happened to her. In this day and age, any news event is quickly pounced on by a couple of people who have access to a microphone and recording devices, and multiple episodes are then released for podcast listeners around the world to download and devour. I found out about the existence of this podcast on social media, a few people referring to it in their comments. "It's really interesting" one of them said. "I'm hooked" said another. It was as if my nightmare had become other people's entertainment, but despite my dismay at that, I still felt compelled to listen to the podcast for myself.

Snatched In Stirling is hosted by a Scottish journalist called Trudy and an English psychologist called Graham and together, the pair discuss what might have happened that fateful night when I last saw my baby. Trudy looks at things more from the police point of view, detailing the investigation so far, while Graham comes at it from the point of view of the kidnapper, whoever they be, describing why a person might take a child and what they could do once they have them. But as well as them using their professional knowledge to discuss the case, they make sure to allow room for some good old- fashioned conspiracy theories and speculation to filter in too, because I guess that leads to more downloads and higher ratings.

I'm on episode four now, and as I press play, I lie back with my head on one of my sofa cushions and prepare to torture myself with the dulcet tones of these two presenters who have figured out a way to profit from my misery.

"Welcome to another episode of Snatched In Stirling, the podcast that explores one of the biggest news stories to strike Scotland in recent years, that being the disappearance of Tuppence Hartley, a six-month-old baby who vanished on a quiet, affluent street in a scenic, low-crime city. I'm Trudy Montgomery, five-time Scottish journalist of the year, and I'm joined, as always, by my companion, Graham Walker, a renowned expert in the field of psychology, in particular, criminal psychology and cases involving children."

The room is starting to spin, so I close my eyes as I listen, hoping that the nauseous feeling I still have in my stomach will settle down soon and I won't have to try and get to the kitchen sink or bathroom toilet in time.

"In previous episodes, we have discussed what might have happened to Tuppence, from her being taken by an opportunistic kidnapper with no prior connection to the child, to her parents and any possible involvement they may have had. Of course, as always, anything we do talk about is only theoretical, and in no way do we make allegations or accusations against any parties. What you will hear are opinions, not facts, and remember that the

police investigation is still ongoing. This podcast is merely for entertainment purposes only."

That's the boring legal bit out of the way, I always think, Trudy having made sure to cover herself and Graham from any potential lawsuits, not that I have the energy or inclination for anything like that at this period in my life.

"In this episode, we'll discuss a theory that was first raised by Tuppence's mother, Gabby, during the public appeal, namely that one of the residents of the street where Tuppence was taken is behind this. That street is Buckingham Place, where the average house price is north of half a million pounds and the most expensive homes are valued at over a million."

As I lie prone on my sofa with my phone on my chest and the podcast continuing to play, my mind drifts back to that dark street and those luxurious homes. Once it does that, I see what I always see when I think about that place. I see one of those residents holding my baby, raising her in secret in a back bedroom, keeping her out of view and well hidden. She's there, I just know it, though all the police searches of the properties failed to find her.

I must drift off into an alcohol-induced stupor then because when I wake up, I check my phone and see that there are only ten minutes left of the podcast. I've missed most of it, and I'll have to skip back in the morning and play it back again to see what was said, but, right now, I hear what is being discussed and it's of great interest to me.

"What do you think about the chatter online about the resident of Buckingham Place who lost a child?" Trudy asks Graham. *"We can't name her here for obvious reasons, but let's just say that there is a theory going around, one that began with an outburst from Tuppence's mother herself on the night of the disappearance, that a resident who lost a child of her own took Tuppence to make up for that."*

"Yes, I am aware of this theory, and it is certainly an interesting one," Graham says, his posh English accent filtering into my home. *"It's obviously common for a parent to want to replace a child they lost with another one and while most people would do this by conceiving again themselves, it's not unheard of for them to resort to more desperate measures, like abduction, for example."*

"There is the case of the mother in Austria who took a baby boy after losing her own."

"Yes, amongst others. It does happen."

"Could it have happened in this case?"

"It's unlikely," Graham says. *"The house has been searched, and nothing untoward was found."*

"What do you say about the theory that Tuppence was taken away from that street and held somewhere for a short while before being smuggled back onto Buckingham Place where she now resides?"

"It's possible, but it would be incredibly risky and a difficult thing to pull off. As many of our listeners will know, having a baby in the house is not an easy thing. Trying to cover up that a baby is there for a long period of time? Impossible, surely."

"The houses are detached and have thick stone walls. The neighbours might not hear if the sound of the baby's cries don't travel."

"That is true, but I think it's unlikely that Tuppence is still on that street. People want her to still be there because it's far less frightening than thinking of her as being in a totally different place, many miles away from where she was last seen."

I'm one of those people who still wants her to be there because Graham is right. It feels better to think of Tuppence as only a few yards away from where I lost her than in a totally different postcode because the country, and the world, is huge, and if she's lost in it, I'll never get her back. Better to think of her in one of those houses, and that's what I still think. These hosts are obviously talking about Raquel, who they can't name, but anyone in the know on this case will be aware of her. I made sure everybody was aware of her by screaming her name in the street. If she's innocent, I'd feel awful, but if she's guilty, she deserves whatever she gets. But the police tell me she is innocent, just like everyone else on that street supposedly is.

The podcast finishes, and as I roll over on the sofa, my phone falls onto the carpet. But I leave it there. I don't need it until dawn. No one will text me or call. Mum thinks I went to bed hours ago, unaware I was actually planning to go out and drink. My friends message occasionally, but it's awkward. I get it, they have their own kids, I'm the elephant in the room, the taboo subject who makes them all feel guilty for still having their children at home safe and well.

As for Leon, he'll only get in touch via his lawyers now. We've begun divorce proceedings, and why waste time? We're going to sell this house and split the proceeds and then that is that.

I pass out then and don't wake up until dawn. When I do, I see I've been sick again, but I don't even care. This house will be somebody else's problem soon, just like Leon will be somebody else's too.

I guess Tuppence falls into that bracket as well. If she's still alive then she's keeping somebody else awake at night, making them feed her every few hours, requiring them to play with her to keep her entertained.

I wish it was me.

All I have to do today is clean up my own mess.

19

You know time has passed and people are getting bored of a certain thing when they stop making podcast episodes about it. Four months is all it has taken for the mystery of my baby's disappearance to stop being the talking point for Trudy and Graham, as well as all their listeners online. Everybody has moved on, seemingly accepting that they won't know what happened, but wasn't it fun to speculate for a while?

Some people can't just move on as easily though. The police, for one, and they are still making enquiries and appeals, looking like they're trying, not getting anywhere but going through the motions. No news, no leads, nothing. I guess the case will always stay open but like the podcast hosts, eventually, Detective Jacobs and his colleagues will find something else to occupy their time with, something that actually gives them results, unlike Tuppence's case, which has just given them a headache.

The residents of Buckingham Place have moved on too, less bothered now by journalists lurking on their doorstep or morbid members of the public trying to visit a crime scene. That's partly down to the fact that they all banded together and hired a security guard to patrol their street and make sure nobody was coming there to bother them, but that security guard has had an easier job now that less people are trying to go there. I heard about the guard online - somebody posted a photo of him telling them to get lost. I remember it made me angry, as if those residents can just pay for security because they're rich, but I was also very drunk when I saw that video, so that might have made my feelings worse. I've been drinking a lot these last four months, far too much, but it was easy to get away with it when I was waking up every day in a house by myself. But it won't be so easy to hide now because I'm moving in with Mum today.

The sale of my family home, the one I shared with Leon and Tuppence and hoped to share with one more child one day, has just been completed. I handed over the keys to the new homeowners this morning and they gratefully took receipt of them, eager to get inside and start unpacking, putting their own stamp on my old place. I wonder what they'll do. Renovate the bedrooms? Fit a new kitchen? Install a new bathroom? Dig up some of the back garden and make a patio? Whatever they decide on, they are free to do it because they are now the rightful owners, and I'm officially homeless because I don't count me moving back in with my mother at my age as anything to be proud of.

The buyers are a couple in their thirties with two kids, and they look like every generic family you've ever seen in your own neighbourhoods. They're so normal and average, right down to the size of the car they drive, the jobs they do and the school they are planning on sending the little ones to. They should have been me, Leon, Tuppence, and Tuppence's future sibling, but we don't get to have what they have anymore. They will go inside the house, and the hardest decision they will make for the rest of the day is which colour should they paint the wall in the back bedroom. I long for their simple life.

As it is, I just handed over the keys, wished them well and walked away to Mum's car, where I cried all the way back to her house.

I did find the time amongst my tears to text Leon and say the house was officially no longer ours, and he replied to thank me for the update and acknowledge that it must have been hard for me to see it go. Not that hard for him, though, because he didn't offer to be there himself, although he would just put that down to the fact that he has moved out of Edinburgh now, having taken a job up near Inverness in the Scottish Highlands, something that he calls a career move but is blatantly just his way of running as far away from his old life as he can. Who can blame him?

With Leon and I divorced and the money from our house sale hitting both of our bank accounts later today, there isn't much else we need to talk about in the future. The only other thing I have reached out to him to discuss lately is what we do on Tuppence's birthday, which is approaching ominously on the horizon. Do we acknowledge it or let it pass? Host some kind of event, release a balloon, make a speech, or just ignore it? I know what Leon's answer will be. He'll bury his head up in the Highlands and pretend it's just another day, and maybe that's for the best. A party will be too sad and a memorial service too final. I'll just say happy birthday to my girl in my head and then probably try and sleep all day.

After unpacking my things at Mum's and coming to grips with the grim realisation of being back in my childhood bedroom for the foreseeable future, my first concern is how I can smuggle alcohol into here every night and drink myself to sleep without her noticing. But she doesn't even allow me the time to figure that out because no sooner do I go downstairs, I find her sitting at the kitchen table, and she has a piece of paper and a pen in front of her.

'I think we need to make a plan,' she says calmly.

'A plan? What for?'

'For you. For your life. Your next steps.'

'I'm too tired for this.'

'You'll always be too tired for it. You've lost a child and you're grieving. But you have to do this or I'll end up losing a child too, and I'm not going to let that happen.'

This has been the way it's been for a little while now. Mum's sympathy for me in the first few months has made way for a type of bluntness that can be shockingly harsh sometimes. I guess it's her way of coping, or it's how she has decided that it's the best way to help me through this time, but it's hard to appreciate it. I'm not asking for pity every day, but I'm certainly not asking for her to be so brutal with me either.

'You're drinking too much,' she tells me. 'Don't pretend you're not because I can smell it on you every time I see you and even if I couldn't, your eyes are a dead giveaway. You look like a zombie, Gabby, and I can't leave you to poison yourself anymore.'

I'm dismayed that I've not done as good a job of keeping my alcoholism under wraps as I'd thought, and my surprise at that allows Mum to get another word in.

'I'm not saying we have to do anything today, or even tomorrow, but we do have to make a plan. You'll have to go back to work at some point. It's great that your employers have granted you compassionate leave, but that won't go on forever, so you need to decide if you want to go back to your old job or get a new one. You also need to decide if you want to stay here or have a change of scene. I would support you either way, and I will move with you if you wish. I understand that you might not want to stay here with old memories. Leon left Edinburgh, and you need to think about if that's the best thing for you to do too.'

This is a lot to take in, far too much for my sleep-deprived brain, but Mum just keeps on going.

'One thing that I think we can both agree on is that you need to stop taking those train rides back to Stirling and wandering around the city,' Mum says, looking terribly sad as she speaks. 'I know you're going because I found old train tickets when I was helping you pack up to move out of your house. And one of my friends saw you boarding a train to Stirling last Tuesday. That was the day you told me you had gone for a walk and visited a counsellor in Edinburgh. But you were lying to me. You went back to Stirling, and you keep going back over and over again.'

'I need to!' I cry. 'I need to check with the police and see what's happening!'

'No, you don't. They keep you informed from here. There's no need for you to keep going back there. What do you think you'll find?'

'I don't know. My missing daughter, maybe!'

Screaming at Mum isn't going to help. It certainly won't help the plan she is supposedly wanting to write down on that piece of paper she has on the table. But I can't handle this. I have to get out of here, so I turn for the front door. But before I can reach it, Mum catches up with me and wraps her arms around me, stopping me from going. That's probably because she knows the first place I will go from here is the pub to drown my sorrows, so she's trying to prevent me from doing that. I resist for a short while, but I'm too tired and weak and soon we're both on the floor, her with her arms around me and me with tears in my eyes. We stay there until I admit that things will change. I will get some professional help. I will make a plan about my future. And I will stop going back to Stirling on the train. Everything I say then is the truth, but there is a small caveat which I don't let Mum in on.

While I will avoid Stirling for the most part, there is a time when I will make an exception and go back. I plan to return to that city on the twelve-month anniversary of Tuppence's disappearance if, heaven forbid, we get that far without any sign of her being discovered.

I have to go back on that date, I just do.

I'll stand in the last spot where I saw her at the exact time when I lost her, and I will say a prayer for my little girl.

It seems so simple in my mind to do such a thing.

What I didn't know then is all the crazy stuff that would happen when I did.

20

The train that takes me back to Stirling on the twelve-month anniversary of Tuppence's vanishing is ten minutes delayed, but that's okay because I've given myself plenty of time to work with. It's still the morning, and I don't have to be on Buckingham Place until 17:22, the exact time my daughter was taken one year ago today. I have a few things to do before then, but really, it feels like all day is just building up to that specific time in the early evening.

The train ride from Edinburgh gives me the time to re-think what I am going to say when I stand outside that house where I last saw my baby, but it's not as if I haven't had plenty of time to consider my words. But I have been busy over these last few months, not just thinking about my daughter but slowly and surely taking Mum's advice and getting my life into some semblance of order.

I decided to stay in Edinburgh because it's my home. There'll always be certain parts of the city that remind me of Tuppence, like anytime I go near the hospital or the place where I used to take her to baby sensory class, but I can limit that. I can also totally avoid going anywhere near my old house, the one where that picture-perfect family now live and are presumably enjoying the property as they go about their lovely lives, free from the type of pain I feel.

Having decided to stay rather than move many miles away like my ex-husband did, the next decision I had to make was work. When would I go back? Would I go back at all? Or would I have a career change? I opted to return to work six months after Tuppence disappeared, just to test it out and see how I found it. What I found immediately upon returning was a lot of love and warmth from my colleagues and that was why I decided that I would keep working there, part-time at first, though now I am back to five days a week in the office. It's actually not bad - it keeps me busy, my mind occupied, and there is the odd minute or two during the day when life feels normal. It doesn't take me long to remember that it's not, but if I do ever shed a tear at my desk, there's always a friendly co-worker on hand to pass me a tissue and fetch me a cup of tea and a biscuit.

As for my current living situation, I used my share of the proceeds of the house sale to buy myself a small flat in a nice area of Edinburgh, walking distance from some shops, restaurants and Mum's place. I take the bus to work, but that's fine because I'm still too distracted to drive, and occasionally, on the weekend, I meet up with a friend but only for food, not drink.

I'm eight months sober now, not having touched a drop of alcohol since I sold the house and cried into Mum's arms on her hallway floor. That 'intervention' she staged for me was a turning point, and looking back now, I'm aware that my mum saved my life.

Too bad I couldn't do the same for my own daughter.

It's not as if I've totally given up on ever finding out what happened to Tuppence. I still dream of the day when some news will come through about somebody seeing her or even that she has been handed in somewhere and is finally ready to be returned to me. It's just that I also have to acknowledge that I might never get her back, and therefore, I have to forge a path that allows me to live somewhat normally rather than end up in an early grave, having abandoned all hope of living. People do just vanish, not only on TV but in real life, and sadly, my daughter is now a statistic, though she will always be far, far more than that to me.

As the train reaches Stirling, which is coated in a frigid February frost, I am not teary, despite having a flashback to when Leon and I had to scramble to get off in time with all our bags back at the start of our fateful holiday. The tears stay away as I leave the station and walk into the centre of the city, losing myself amongst the locals and tourists, the sight of several shopping bags on the street letting me know that for everyone else here, this really is just another day. I buy a coffee and take my time drinking it, before I'm on the move again, this time headed for the police station, where I have an appointment with a certain detective.

Jacobs looks well when I see him, having lost a bit of weight around his waistline in comparison to the time we made the public appeal together. I wonder what prompted his diet. Perhaps it was seeing himself on television, or maybe he simply felt like a change. I know the feeling. But I don't ask him what his new exercise regime might be, allowing him to ask me how I have been getting on since we were last together.

'I'm okay,' I say, which is actually an honest answer because I am okay, aren't I? I'm surviving, anyway.

'Okay, so this is where we are up to,' Jacobs says after he has invited me to take a seat in a small room with him where we can get a little privacy.

As I watch him open a folder, I prepare to receive an update on my daughter's case. Sadly, I'm already aware there isn't much in the way of news.

'Unfortunately, as you know, there were no cameras on Buckingham Place or any of the smaller, surrounding streets. But, as we told you before, my officers analysed all the CCTV footage from the main roads in the area, and we have spoken to any vehicle owners who were seen driving in the vicinity of Buckingham Place, visiting them all at their homes and checking for any signs of your child. It's taken a while to get through everybody, but we have done it.'

'If that didn't turn anything up, doesn't it tell you that Tuppence wasn't driven from the scene but actually stayed close by?'

'You know my thoughts on this theory. We've searched every house on that street and the neighbouring streets. You also know how much hassle it has caused for us to be able to do that. Not many people enjoy having their homes turned upside down when they haven't done anything wrong.'

I promised myself that I wouldn't get annoyed or frustrated, so I take on board what Jacobs is saying before we move on.

'Because it's the anniversary, we will be releasing the image of what we think Tuppence might look like now. That could result in some information coming to light, so let's be hopeful there.'

I have already seen that created image of Tuppence as an eighteen-month-old and while I'm not convinced that it is what she looks like these days, I know it's not an easy thing to imagine a baby's development without any actual photos to go on.

'We will also take you to make your statement to the press when you are ready,' Jacobs goes on. 'They're waiting in the media room now.'

With little else to add, I tell Jacobs that I'm ready and he leads me to where the journalists are poised, and as they turn their cameras on, I take out my prepared statement and begin reading.

'It's been one year since my little girl was taken, and not a day has gone by when I haven't wished to be reunited with her. I know that might not be possible now, but whatever has happened, I just want to find out who did this and why. Somebody out there must know something. If you do, please call the number on the bottom of your screen. Don't think any detail is too small or insignificant. Please, I just want to know what happened to my little girl.'

With that, my part of this anniversary public appeal is complete, and now, Jacobs is talking. He could have had to wait a little longer for his turn to speak if Leon had accepted the invitation to come here and say a few words himself, but he chose not to. I wonder what he'll be doing today to mark this date. I wonder if he'll even see this on the news later. The only thing I don't wonder about is if he still loves me.

Once the public appeal is over, I thank the detective for his help so far, part of my plan to be more composed and respectful these days rather than wild and impulsive, not that either course of action seems to have made much difference in finding Tuppence. Then I head back into the city, wandering around, getting a bite to eat, and I eventually find myself at the castle, where the view helps lift my mood slightly. But as the pale winter sun begins to set and darkness falls, my mood darkens with it and that's because I'm now on my way to Buckingham Place.

I get there just after five and walk around to kill some time, looking at all the houses I pass by, imagining I'll catch a glimpse of my daughter in one of them, sitting in a highchair at a table or perhaps toddling around, enjoying her new-found ability to move herself without the help of others. Even if I get her back now, I've already missed so many developmental milestones, but there's still so many more I could witness if I get lucky and spot her. But I don't, probably because everybody else is right.

She is not on Buckingham Place.

At the appropriate time, I come to a stop outside the house where I heard the woman calling for help that night. But all is quiet on this night, not a single sound to be heard, and how I wish that had been the case twelve months ago. If so, I would have walked right on by this house with the pram before taking Tuppence home for her bath.

It's not long before I regret coming here because as my brain is flooded with flashbacks, I start to lose the fragile grip I had on reality, and it's not long before I'm considering ruining my sobriety. The fact I leave Buckingham Place and go straight to a pub is an indicator that my willpower crumbled, and after several drinks, I felt like I was back at square one again.

That was when one of the other drinkers in the pub, a man with scraggly hair and a scruffy-looking jacket, approached me and asked if I wanted to go home with him.

I sensed danger immediately and should have said no.

But I was past the point of caring.

So I said yes.

That's when part two of Tuppence's disappearance began.

21

When I open my eyes, I fail to recognise my surroundings. This is not my bedroom or any bedroom I have ever been in before, and that realisation, coupled with my throbbing headache, makes me start to panic.

As I nervously check beneath the duvet to see if I am dressed, it's a relief to discover I'm not naked, but I still don't know whose house I am in. I decide I don't want to find out while I'm lying in their bed, so I get up as quickly as I can, scooping up my coat and putting it on to go with the blouse and jeans I apparently slept in. Then I find my shoes by the closed bedroom door and put them on too, but before I leave, I notice something. It's a large pinboard on the wall opposite my bed and when I take a closer look at it, I notice there are several concerning words written on the pieces of paper that are pinned to it.

First victim.

The killer.

What happened to the child?

What the hell is this place, and whose home am I in? I have no idea, but I'm ready to get out of here and head for the door as quickly as I can.

But who will I bump into on my way?

Nervously reaching for the door, I rack my brains as I try to remember who I might have met and ended up with. My hangover tells me I drank lots, as does my foggy memory, and it's the latter that prevents me from figuring this out. Then I bite the bullet and open the bedroom door, preparing to 'meet' whoever brought me back here.

'Good morning,' says the handsome Scottish man in the smart, blue sweater at the other end of the hallway.

As I left one room, he was just leaving another, and I assume that room he has just come out of was where he slept. Or at least I hope it was.

This must be the guy I met whilst drinking last night. I have a vague memory of talking to somebody in a pub. Did I approach him? Did we kiss? Did we do anything else?

'I imagine you have a lot of questions,' the man says with a soft smile that somehow manages to calm a few of my anxieties. 'I'll answer two of them for you now. My name is Cameron, and no, we didn't sleep together last night.'

It's good to know that, as well as get this man's name, although I'm still unclear how I ended up here, even if we weren't intimate with each other.

'Did we meet in a pub?' I ask, ashamed that I can't remember our introduction myself.

'We did,' Cameron says. 'But it was a little unusual. You were actually leaving with somebody else before I managed to stop you.'

'Somebody else?'

'Yes, a guy by the name of Ralph. Everybody in Stirling knows Ralph. He's the guy who uses his disability money from the government to get drunk all day. He's also the guy who can be a bit of a menace to the fairer sex, if you know what I mean. That's why I intervened. I saw he was trying to take advantage of you and stepped in. I hope you don't mind, but I'm pretty sure I saved you from a nasty experience.'

'Oh, okay,' I say, really wishing I could remember it all so I could form my own opinion on that. But as far as I can tell, I'm safe and well, and Cameron is being friendly to me, so I guess everything is alright.

'Would you like some breakfast?' he asks me then. 'I don't have much in, but I could make toast. Or I could go and grab a bagel?'

'Erm, no, I'm okay, thank you. I better be going,' I say, figuring it's best to just remove myself from this awkward situation as quickly as possible.

I head for the stairs then, but Cameron follows me down.

'Are you sure you're okay?' he asks me. 'You didn't seem okay last night.'

'What do you mean?' I ask him as I reach the bottom of the stairs. I'm close to the front door now, but I'd be foolish to ignore any further insight into what happened last night.

'Look, I'll be honest with you,' Cameron says. 'I know who you are and what you've been through.'

'Sorry, what?'

'Your daughter. Tuppence. You're her mother, right?'

My silence is his answer.

'I didn't realise it was you at first. Like I said, I was just trying to keep you away from Ralph. But when we got outside the pub, I recognised you, and I asked if you were okay. That was when you started crying and told me you needed help.'

Oh God, that sounds embarrassing. But it also sounds like me.

'You said you thought you could move on with your life but you can't, and that you're convinced your daughter is still alive and can be rescued, if only you can find her. Then you said you think Buckingham Place holds the key. You wanted to go back there last night, but I stopped you.'

'I did?'

'Yeah, you were pretty determined to go there, and you said you were going to start banging on doors until somebody told you the truth. I managed to stop you, as I feared you'd get arrested. There was a taxi there, so I invited you back to mine so we could talk. You refused at first but then admitted you had nowhere else to stay because you had missed your train back to Edinburgh. So you came back here.'

'What happened then?'

'Nothing. You fell asleep in the taxi. I woke you back up, helped you inside and put you to bed and that was it.'

I look at Cameron and his sweater and then at the fairly modest home he lives in and think about how this man most likely saved me from making a very big mistake last night, either with Ralph or if I had made it back to that street.

'Thank you,' I tell him. 'I mean, I honestly can't remember any of it, but thank you.'

'No problem,' Cameron says. 'Now, you can leave if you like, but it's early and I don't know where you'd go. Or you can take a seat on my sofa, and I'll be back in ten minutes with a breakfast bagel and a cup of coffee for you. How does that sound?'

It sounds good, far better than me wandering around outside again, so I nod my head and go and find the sofa in question while Cameron puts his coat on and heads out for breakfast.

As I wait for him to return, I look around his small living room, noting the overflowing bookcase and pads of paper on his coffee table and assume he's some kind of a writer. Either that or he just loves to read. That would actually make sense considering what I found on the wall in his spare bedroom, and sure enough, a moment later, I find a book on a shelf and the author's first name is Cameron. I read the blurb on the back, and it sounds like the story is about a Scottish detective who is trying to solve the mystery of his ex-wife's disappearance whilst battling a crippling alcohol addiction. Not exactly original stuff, which may be why I've never heard of this book or seen it in the supermarket.

Feeling nosy still, I flick through the pages and read a few snippets of text, getting a glimpse of all sorts of plot points like car chases, sordid affairs and the poisoning of a former lover. It's all very random and a little chaotic without full context, so I put the book back where I found it before I check out his kitchen and dining room. I see they are equally as small and equally as untidy, and when I peep out of the living room window, I notice we are on a street full of terraced houses.

Buckingham Place, this is not.

Cameron is back as promptly as he promised and after he has handed me breakfast, I thank him for his continued kindness before tucking into the bagel and giving my fatigue a jolt with the coffee. Once I'm feeling a little more human, I ask Cameron about himself, if only to avoid us talking about me for a little longer.

'So you noticed all the notepads full of bad handwriting?' he says with a laugh after I have asked him if he is some kind of author. 'I hope you didn't pick any of them up and read from them. It would probably be the worst writing you've ever seen.'

'I didn't read anything,' I say honestly, and he seems relieved about that.

'I am an author, or at least I try to be,' he tells me. 'I have a publisher, but they're small and pretty useless. Let's just say I won't be popping up on any bestseller lists any time soon.'

'Oh, I'm sure you're very good at what you do,' I reply politely.

Cameron appreciates the compliment, though he knows I'm just being nice because I've never read any of his work.

'That's the polite summary of my career,' he says. 'But the reality is, my books aren't great because my ideas aren't great, and that, mixed in with a publisher who isn't great, means overall, I'm fortunate to be scraping a living at this.'

'I'm sure it's not that bad,' I say as I pick up one of his books that lies on a side table.

'Are you a crime fiction fan?' Cameron asks me before realising he might have just made a mistake. 'Sorry, forget that. Of course you're not after what happened.'

'No, it's okay,' I say. 'I tend to avoid crime stories these days for obvious reasons, but this looks good.'

'You're probably only the tenth person to pick up a copy of that book,' Cameron says with a self-deprecating chuckle. 'Me and my mother picked up the other nine.'

I smile then before putting the book down, and there's a brief silence between us. But it's not particularly awkward, and I'm glad things aren't as difficult as they were when I first woke up here. But what last night has taught me, or at least what I was told about last night, is what I have been feeling in my gut for a long time. No matter how much I try and pretend that I can get on with my life and wait for the police to give me some news, I'm living a lie.

It only took one night of losing control for me to realise the truth.

I am going to have to get to the bottom of what happened to Tuppence myself.

'What's your plan?' Cameron asks me as if reading my mind, although thankfully, he can't actually do that because if he did, he would be shocked at what I was thinking.

'I'm going to stay in Stirling for a little while,' I reply. 'I'll take some time off work. It's weird, but I feel closer to my daughter when I'm here.'

'You said that last night,' Cameron says with a sad smile. 'You think she's still here somewhere, don't you?'

'Maybe,' I reply.

'Well, if you need a place to stay while you're here, you're welcome to sleep in my spare bedroom again. I'm guessing you found the bed comfortable enough. I heard your snoring through the walls.'

'Oh no, I don't want to disrupt your life any more than I have done. I can get a hotel.'

'Nonsense. It's no disruption, at least not for a procrastinating writer like me. Besides, I could do with the company.'

I'm guessing from that statement that Cameron is lonely, and I realise then that I didn't see any photos of any partner or children when I was having a snoop around his home earlier while he was out.

'I'm widowed,' he tells me, and now it's my turn to be sympathetic to him.

'I'm so sorry,' I say before looking around because I would have expected there to be a photo of his wife somewhere here if he used to have one.

'You're wondering why I don't have any photos up?' he says then, pre-empting me. 'I did for a while, but it was too painful to see her face every day.'

I know what he means. I try not to spend too long looking at photos of Tuppence these days or I just end up spiralling.

'She passed away two years ago. Cancer. What else?' he says with a sad shrug. 'So it's just me here now. Well, me and my terribly written stories, so if you can put up with either of them, you are very welcome to stay.'

I laugh then, and for the life of me, I can't remember when the last time I did that was. I've faked plenty of smiles since I've been around friends and colleagues over the past few months, but that was a genuine moment of happiness. That's why I accept the invitation to stay here for as long as I decide to remain in Stirling.

'Okay, the bad news is, now you've finished your bagel, there isn't any more food in the house unless I go shopping,' Cameron says as he crumples up his own bagel wrapper in his hands. 'But the good news is, as a writer, I'm free all day to do whatever I want, including helping you if you need me to. So, tell me, Gabby. What do you want to do?'

I crumple up my own bagel wrapper and take the last sip of my coffee before I give Cameron my answer. I tell him that right now, I just need a walk by myself to clear my head.

But I'm lying to him.

I'm not planning on simply going for a walk.

I am planning on going to Buckingham Place.

In particular, I am planning on going to Raquel's house.

22

I leave Cameron's terraced home and make my way along the icy streets of Stirling. As I go, the houses on either side of the roads I walk down become bigger and more prestigious until I eventually make it to the grandest street of them all.

Pausing by the sign for *Buckingham Place* that sits on the corner of the road, I linger behind a hedge, out of view of Raquel if she was to come to her window and look out. But there's no sign of her at any of the windows, so I quickly move closer until I am on her driveway. Then I rush down the side of her house, opening the gate before closing it behind me so that everything looks as it should. Hopefully, nobody saw me sneak down here, especially the homeowner.

There's a window on the side of the house but it's made of frosted glass, so I'm guessing it's a downstairs bathroom. I duck under it just in case Raquel is in there and sees my shadow go past before I reach the back garden. Any outdoor furniture that is used here in summer is currently under wraps to protect it from the winter frost, and there isn't much to see. But I'm hoping I'll see a lot more when I take a peek through the window a few yards away from me and after cautiously approaching it, I peer inside.

I see a kitchen, and it's a very luxurious one at that, all marble worktops and shiny pots and pans. I also see a highchair by the breakfast bar, as well as the messy remnants of what appears to have been a child's meal.

Raquel's daughter, Lexi, must be just over a year and a half old, as she was practically the same age as Tuppence, so that means proper food for her these days, not just the bottles of milk the two babies were enjoying the last time I saw this woman.

But as I stare at the highchair, I wonder – is it just Lexi who has sat in there? Or has Tuppence been in there too? Fuelled by the memory of the way Raquel seemed enamoured with my child when we met in the pub, I am desperate to get inside this house and find out if somehow, the woman who lives here has orchestrated a scenario where she has the two babies she should have had instead of just one. But I can't just walk in if she's in there. I have to be smart and wait until she goes out, so I sneak back around to the front of the house and linger by the side gate.

It's fifteen minutes later when I hear a noise inside the house. It's the sound of a baby crying, and two minutes later, I hear a front door open, and the crying gets louder. Standing on a plant pot, I use the extra height to peer over the top of the gate and when I do, I see Raquel pushing a pram out of her house.

I can't see the baby inside it, only hear it, but I have to assume it's Lexi. Even if Raquel did take Tuppence, she wouldn't be stupid enough to go walking around Stirling with her. She would leave her inside, out of view, which is why I fully intend to get inside this house just as soon as Raquel has disappeared down the street.

I wait for Raquel's footsteps and the sound of her crying baby to quieten as they move away before I venture out from my hiding place, and then I get to work looking for any spare keys that might be hidden around the exterior of the house. I check under plant pots and rockery but no luck there, but everyone has a hidden key somewhere, don't they? Then I snoop around the shed in the back garden, but nothing there either. It's only when I kneel down and take a peek under the covered furniture that I see a small key lying on the patio and after pulling it out, I head for the back door to give it a try.

The key slots in easily.

I'm in.

Not caring about the fact that I've just committed a crime, I enter the house and look around. I've already had a pretty good look at the kitchen from the outside, so I move through there quickly and go into the hallway. But there's not much to see in here, so I go through another door and that's when I realise that I'm in a playroom.

There are chests full of toys and shelves full of books and even a tepee in the corner, which I guess is what Lexi uses as a little den. This is the kind of room I imagined creating for Tuppence as she grew, somewhere she could have as her own to let her imagination run wild and play. But is she the only child who plays in here or is there another one, one who shouldn't be here?

I leave the playroom and go into the adjoining room, which is a lounge area. The sofas are large and expensive looking, just like the television and the rest of the furniture in here. The next room is the dining room, but it's pretty sparse in here, free of any child's belongings, which is almost impressive because usually, once a baby arrives, every room in the home is infiltrated with their things.

Heading for the stairs, I'm aware I'll be totally screwed if Raquel comes back and I'm up there because I won't be able to escape easily, but I can't leave here without having a proper check around. If I really think Raquel might have taken Tuppence, I owe it to my daughter to search thoroughly.

Reaching the upper floor, I push open some of the doors and see a bathroom and a master bedroom. But I'm looking for a child's bedroom and when I find it, I gasp because there are two beds in here.

If Raquel only has Lexi, why does she need two beds?

Unless she has my baby too?

'Tuppence?' I call out, rushing around the rest of the rooms upstairs, but there is no sign of her. I find a bathtub with some toys in it and a wardrobe full of toddler clothes, but that's it as far as baby stuff goes.

Going back downstairs, I'm wondering what I can do next when I notice a door that I must have missed the first time I passed through this hallway.

I immediately go to it and try the handle, but it's locked.

That's when I hear the sound of a baby crying.

23

My first thought is to kick down this door because my baby is obviously on the other side of it and needs her mother. But then I realise the sound is coming from behind another door.

It's the front door.

Raquel is back.

Realising that I can hear Lexi's cries and not Tuppence's, I panic and rush to the back door because I need to get out of here before I'm caught or I'll be back at the police station again, but not on my own terms. But in my haste to get away before Raquel sees me, I get my coat caught on the kitchen door handle, and as I try to free myself, I hear the front door open, and Lexi's cries get louder.

'It's okay, baby. We're home again now. It's Mummy's fault for trying to take you out when you were due a feed.'

Raquel sounds as weary as any mother of a toddler would be, but she also sounds incredibly close, and all she has to do is walk a few more yards into her home and she will see me desperately trying to free my coat from where it is stuck on the handle.

'Let's get you some food then,' Raquel says in between Lexi's cries, and I guess feeding time means kitchen time, so Raquel will be in here any second.

I finally manage to get my coat free and rush to the back door, but I fear I'm not going to make it in time, and I'll be seen leaving the house. Then I hear a knock at the front door, and whoever it is has just bought me several precious seconds.

As Raquel answers the front door, I leave via the back one and quickly lock up before returning the key to its hiding place. Then I rush around the side of the house and only pause when I reach the gate. Then I peer over it to see what is going on at the front of the property.

That's when I see Cameron standing on the driveway.

'Are you sure? I could have sworn this was the address I was given,' he says as he scratches his head and looks around.

'Sorry, there's no one here by that name,' I hear Raquel reply, before Cameron shrugs his shoulders and apologises. Then he wishes Raquel a good day before turning and walking away, and as Raquel closes the door, I know I'm safe to leave my hiding place now.

I also know that Cameron just saved me from getting caught.

I catch up to him on the corner of Buckingham Place when we're both out of sight of Raquel's house and when I do, I ask him what the hell just happened.

'I had a feeling you were going to do something stupid,' Cameron says. 'You were so fired up last night outside that pub, talking about this street and how you knew Raquel was hiding something, that I just knew you weren't simply going for a walk today. You were coming here. What the hell were you thinking? You could have been arrested?'

'I can't believe you followed me!'

'It's a good job I did, isn't it? Raquel came back early from her walk, and she nearly walked in on you. What would have happened then? How would you have explained yourself?'

'I don't know,' I admit as I look back in the direction of her house. 'I just-'

'Wasn't thinking?'

Cameron is clearly stunned that I could do something so reckless as break into a house in the middle of the day, but to me, at least at the time, it made perfect sense.

'She's hiding something,' I say, still convinced of it. 'There are two cribs in the baby's bedroom, and there's a locked door in her house. I guess it leads to a basement. I couldn't get in there, but I need to.'

'What are you talking about? You think your daughter is in some basement? Are you serious?'

'Yes!'

'But the police searched all these homes.'

'I know, but what if they missed something?'

'They missed a crying baby?'

I shake my head at Cameron because he just doesn't get it, or at least I think he doesn't until he tells me that we need to talk about this and suggests we go for something to eat. I'm not sure I can concentrate on food with the adrenaline still coursing around my body after what just happened, but I do owe Cameron one after he saved me, so I follow him until we are sitting in a café. Then, after we have each ordered a sandwich and a soft drink, he tells me what he thinks I should do next.

'I understand you have to do something to look for your daughter, but you have to be smarter about it,' he says as I watch a waitress taking two cups of tea over to a neighbouring table. 'What you're doing would be like me just launching head-first into writing a book without any idea where the story is going. I'll make some mistakes along the way, but I'll make less if I plot it out and plan ahead. So that's what you need to do.'

'What do you mean?'

'You need to plan ahead. If you think somebody on that street has your baby, whether it's in that house you searched or somewhere else, you need to know the people you are looking into. The suspects, as it were. The more you know about them, the more you can figure out who fits the profile most.'

'Raquel fits the profile!'

'Okay, she's obviously your prime suspect. But based on what I read about this case, there were two people involved in this kidnapping.'

'Two?'

'Well, yeah. The woman who was calling out for help and then her accomplice. I mean, somebody had to have been watching you to know when you were outside that house. They would have called that woman and told her to start crying out for help. So to me, that suggests it is a couple who are behind this. Or two friends.'

A couple?

'Raquel is on her own,' I say, thinking out loud.

'So maybe it isn't her,' Cameron replies as our drinks are served to us.

'It could have been a friend, like you said.'

'Could have been. Or it could be two people who live on that street or nearby it. Two people who saw Tuppence being pushed along in her pram in that area over the past few nights and who decided to seize an opportunity to take your child.'

Cameron seems to have spent some time coming up with his own theories about this, and as I stare at him, he realises what I'm thinking.

'Hey, I'm a crime writer,' he says with a chuckle. 'What kind of crime writer would I be if I hadn't given some serious thought to the biggest crime that's happened in my city for a long time?'

That's true, and as our sandwiches are served, I realise Cameron and his inquisitive mind might be able to help me more.

'So what can I do?' I ask, feeling pretty helpless as another day ticks by without knowing if my daughter is okay.

'You have to be methodical about it,' Cameron replies as he inspects his sandwich. 'You make profiles of your suspects. People on that street who could have seen what happened. Which houses have vantage points of that house you stopped outside of? Do any have views of the front and back of that property? Where do the possible escape routes lead to? I'm not sure what happened, but I think you're right about one thing. Somebody around there saw something – there are simply too many houses for nobody to have caught a glimpse of your baby being taken. We just have to figure out who it is and why they're hiding it.'

Cameron is clearly enthused at the task that lies ahead of us, or maybe it's just because this is more interesting to him than going back to writing whichever book he is currently having trouble finishing. Either way, he's willing to help and has some ideas how to go about that, so I might as well use his enthusiasm. Perhaps he also realises that such a project will help occupy my mind, and feeling sorry for me after my drunken outbursts last night, he's trying to keep me busy, at least until I realise that we've tried everything, and only then might I be able to properly move on with my life.

We could just be two lonely people looking for something to take our minds off our miserable lives, but even if we are, we have each other now, so as we eat our sandwiches, we talk about what we'll do next. By the time we're finished with lunch, I am feeling a little better about things, if only because it's all been a distraction from going back to my normal life. I guess that's the same thing Cameron needed too.

Now the pair of us are working together.

Let's see if we can do what the police couldn't.

Let's see if we can find the truth.

24

'I usually use this for plotting out my books,' Cameron says as he leads me into his spare bedroom and points at the wall. 'But I figure it'll work for what we need it for here.'

I stare at the huge pinboard fixed to the wall and all the coloured pins that stick out of it. There are currently several pieces of paper stuck to the board with various bits of writing on them saying things like 'The Midpoint' and 'The Third Act Twist', which is all authorly speak for constructing a story. But Cameron quickly takes all of those down and puts them in a neat pile before pointing at his now empty pinboard.

'Let's recreate that street and that night,' he says as he picks up a few pins and a blank sheet of paper.

'This is you and your baby,' he says, drawing me and a pram on the paper before pinning it in the centre of the board. 'And these are the houses on that street.'

Cameron quickly draws several sketches of houses before pinning them in position so that it looks like a street, and I help him get them all in the right place with my now-microscopic knowledge of that place.

'Okay, from this, we can see which houses had a good view of you and your baby,' Cameron says, and he uses bits of string to connect those houses that were in viewing distance of me and Tuppence that night.

'That's Raquel's house,' I say, stepping forward and writing her name on the relevant piece of paper. 'I know who lives in these ones too.'

I write titles like 'Old Man' and 'Neighbour Who Called The Police' on another couple of houses, as well as using my memory to fill in a few more of the blanks.

'Okay, so there are a couple of houses where we don't know who lives there,' Cameron summarises as he studies the board. 'We can do a little reconnaissance work there and plug those gaps. But we also need to look a little further afield because the police already searched these homes and found nothing.'

'Further afield?'

'Yes, neighbouring streets, like what about the one adjacent to Buckingham Place? It could still have been close enough for somebody to take your child and get them home. Those houses there weren't searched until the day after, so Tuppence could have been moved or better hidden in that time.'

Cameron uses his phone to bring up a map of the area around Buckingham Place and then sticks a few more sheets of paper on to represent more houses. Then, as he uses his string to connect them to the image of me and Tuppence, he notices something.

'This house here had a direct line of sight to the spot where you stopped with the pram,' Cameron says, running his fingers along the piece of string until it ends at a house on the bend of the road adjacent to Buckingham Place.

I step closer again and study it and see that Cameron is right.

'They would have seen me approaching Buckingham Place with the pram,' I say. 'They would also have seen me stop outside that house. If somebody ran out then, they could have got Tuppence back to the property in what? Ten seconds?'

'Yeah, I guess,' Cameron says. 'It's interesting that this house wouldn't have been searched until the day after because if you look at this map, it's practically as close to the scene where she vanished as most of the houses actually on Buckingham Place,' Cameron muses. 'So it escaped being searched that first night simply because it technically wasn't on the same street. But distance wise, it's the same.'

'We need to go and look at that house,' I decide quickly, and Cameron is in agreement, so we leave the pinboard behind and head out, quickly walking to where we need to go and staying dry in the process because the weather is fair in Stirling today.

'Thank you,' I say to Cameron as we walk.

'What for?'

'For helping me. For humouring me. Whatever it is you're doing. It feels like everybody else in this city has forgotten about my daughter and moved on. They might not say it, the police certainly won't admit it, but it sure feels that way. My ex-husband has moved on too. New job in a new place. Even my mother told me to stop dwelling on the past and look forward. You've been the only person so far who seems to understand that it's impossible to move on.'

'Maybe it's the writer in me,' Cameron says. 'But I can put myself into other people's shoes and when I put myself in yours, it makes perfect sense that you'd want to search every house in this city - every house in Scotland - until you found out where your daughter was.'

I smile at Cameron as we approach Buckingham Place, but for once, I am not walking onto that street. I'm stopping at the house on the corner that overlooks it.

It's another impressive property made of sturdy stone - detached and with a sizeable front garden, and it's set back a little way from the road, giving it more privacy. This house might actually be worth even more than some of those on Buckingham Place and I'm intrigued as to who lives here but only because they could be involved in my daughter's disappearance.

As Cameron realised, this house does have a perfect view of the spot where Tuppence was taken. I would have walked right past here only a few moments before I stopped outside that house.

'Let's go and see who lives here,' I say, heading for the door, but Cameron tells me to slow down.

'Wait, maybe we should just watch for a little while. Walk around. Not make it obvious that we're spying.'

'Why wait? Let's see who is home,' I say, and Cameron already knows me well enough to be aware of my stubbornness, so he allows me to keep moving.

'What are you going to say when they answer?' he asks me as we reach the door.

'I don't know. I'll see what they have to say. Maybe they won't say anything when they realise who I am.'

I knock then and as I wait, I look behind me at Buckingham Place. This house really is close.

But there's no answer, and after knocking two more times, I'm resigned to admit that no one is home. Not yet anyway.

'We can wait,' I say as I walk away. 'Let's take a walk around. We might see something.'

Cameron and I spend the next hour wandering the streets in and around Buckingham Place, and my head is on a swivel, turning and looking into every home I pass, every car window that drives by and every garden that is full of trees and neatly trimmed hedges. Being here makes me feel like Tuppence is close again and I never know where I might see her. But I haven't seen her after we have finished our walk and got back to where we started, although I do see something of interest.

A car is parking on the driveway of the house we are interested in, and I watch as a man in his forties gets out before he heads for the door. But just as he gets there, it opens and a woman of a similar age smiles as she welcomes him in.

And she has a female toddler in her arms.

'Tuppence!' I cry as I rush towards the house, convinced that woman is holding my child. She must have been in the house the whole time and chose not to answer the door when I knocked, which is suspect in itself, but now I have seen her, I know what she is hiding.

The woman looks up at me and seems shocked to see me, as does her partner, who instinctively steps in front of his family to shield them from the approaching stranger. But he's merely blocking me from my daughter, and despite Cameron trying to slow me down by grabbing for my arm, I reach the front door.

'Tuppence!' I shout, and now she starts crying, my baby girl, the one who was stolen from me. She's upset and of course she is because she just wants her mother, and her mother is not the woman who is currently holding on to her.

'Give me back my baby!' I cry, my arms outstretched as I lunge for the woman, but her partner prevents me from getting any closer, putting his hands on my shoulders and keeping me back. As he slows me down, the woman with my baby retreats into her home, and I've lost sight of Tuppence once again, but now I know she is near, I am not going to let her vanish again.

'Call the police!' I instruct Cameron, who is trying to tell both me and the man restraining me to calm down. 'Call them and get them here quick before these people can get away with this again!'

'What are you talking about?' the male homeowner says as he tries to push me away, but I just move forward again and he realises I'm not going to stop, which is why he rushes into his house and slams the door behind him so I can't follow him in. But I just pound on the door and keep calling out my baby's name until I see that Cameron hasn't done as I asked and called the police yet.

'I'll call them then!' I cry as I get my phone.

'Just wait a minute. What if you're wrong? What if these people are innocent?' he tries, but I ignore him until I'm speaking to an operator.

'Yes, I need the police as quickly as possible. I'm on the corner of Buckingham Place. It's about the kidnapping of Tuppence Hartley. I've caught the people who have her!'

25

I've been reunited with Detective Jacobs again, although he doesn't look particularly thrilled to see me. Maybe that's because I've just done what he and his team failed to do and find my daughter and the people who took her.

'Calm down,' Jacobs says to me after I have just banged my hands on the table between us for the third time since our conversation began.

'I can't calm down! That couple have my baby and you aren't believing me!' I cry, desperately defiant. 'Arrest them and have a DNA test done! Do it now!'

The detective sits back in his seat, possibly to put a bit more distance between him and my exasperated pleas, but I give him no time to talk me out of this.

'Just do the test! If that couple have nothing to hide then they won't refuse it, will they? If it's their baby, they'll have the test done. But it's not their baby, it's mine!'

'What is this?' Jacobs asks, throwing his hands up. 'You think every child in Stirling who is the same age as Tuppence would be now is her? Is that it?'

'No, of course not! But their house is so close to where she was taken. They could have seen everything and planned it. They knew we walked past there at the same time every night, and they could have worked together to steal her. She distracted me and he took Tuppence and smuggled her back to their house, which is only a few seconds away. Then they hid her, I don't know where, but they did, and ever since then, they've gotten away with this. Until today!'

Jacobs still looks like I'm talking nonsense, but I've never been so sure of anything in my life.

'You didn't search their house that first night, did you?' I ask him, and the detective has to admit that he did not.

'That doesn't mean they have your child,' he adds. 'Do you know how I know that?'

'How?'

'Because their child, a girl called Felicity, was born at Stirling General Hospital on the 31st August, months before Tuppence went missing in the following February. How could they have faked that? There were several midwifes who witnessed them having a child!'

I don't know what to say to that and Jacobs shakes his head at me as I ponder it.

'You've just accused two innocent people of being kidnappers. How do you think they feel about that? Let me tell you, they're not happy, and I wouldn't be surprised if they didn't try to sue you for causing emotional distress to them and their child.'

'I don't know…I thought-'

'You thought they had your baby. Well, they don't, and you've just wasted their time as well as ours. What are you doing here, Gabby? I know you've been through hell and you're probably still there, but you can't be doing this. Any more stunts like what you pulled today and I'll have to arrest you for public disturbance and harassment.'

'Arrest me? But I've done nothing wrong! It's my baby that has been taken! Why am I being made out to be the bad guy here?'

'Because you aren't getting it, are you?' Jacobs cries, his hands up in the air for a second time. 'My colleagues and I will never stop trying to find your daughter, but we may never achieve that. Therefore, you may never know what happened to her. I'm truly sorry about that, believe me, I am, but you cannot spend the rest of your life accusing strangers of a serious crime. The only one who will suffer will be you when you're in prison. No one else.'

I don't know what to say to that, but I do start crying, which makes Jacobs calm down a bit. He's lowered his voice a lot by the time he speaks again.

'Tuppence wouldn't want you to be like this,' he says, and I look up at him with tears in my eyes. 'You should try and make her proud. She'd want you to try and be happy.'

'How do you know what she would want? All she wants is me.'

'Just think about it,' Jacobs says as he stands up to leave, but he pushes a box of tissues towards me before he goes, showing he isn't being uncaring, just a bit blunt.

'And do yourself a favour. Stop hanging around with a guy who writes crime fiction for a living,' Jacobs says, causing me to frown. 'Yes, I'm talking about Cameron Cargill. I recognised him with you when you came in here, and I know him well. He's often bombarding my colleagues for interviews, wanting insight into police work to help him with his writing, but generally, just making our jobs harder. I expect he's filled your head with all sorts of fantastical theories, half of them most likely straight from the plots of all his books that haven't sold. I don't think a person like him is healthy to be around for a person like you.'

Jacobs leaves the room then, but I stay in there for half an hour, crying, drying my eyes and then crying again, but I eventually force myself to leave and when I do, I find Cameron waiting for me.

'What's going on?' he asks me, concern etched on his face. 'What did the detective say?'

'It's not Tuppence,' I tell him as I wipe my eyes, the bright lights overhead in this part of the police station stinging them a little. 'I'm wrong. They don't have my baby.'

Cameron looks sorry for me, and I've been used to receiving such expressions for a while now. I decide not to tell him about what Jacobs said about him, mainly because it wasn't particularly complimentary, and there's no point hurting the man who has been trying to help me. Cameron continues to help me as he takes me back to his place, and as dusk falls, I tell him I'm going to go and have a lie down in the bedroom that has become my temporary home.

As I lie on the mattress and stare at the pinboard on the wall, my eyes follow all the strings and I find it impossible to rest in here. But it's not just because I'm trying to sleep in a room containing a wallchart of my baby's abduction. It's because despite the drama and chaos of the day, I can't rest, not when I'm still thinking about that couple's baby. Jacobs said that girl was born six months before Tuppence went missing. That would make her the same age as my daughter.

What if that couple lost their original child in that time and, distraught and devastated, saw a way to replace the baby they had lost? There could have been an accident at home, or they woke up one morning before February to find their baby lifeless, and what if, instead of just reporting it and facing their grief, they saw me walking past their house with a pram and realised there was a chance to fill their home with a baby's love again?

It might be a reflection of my increasingly unhinged state of mind that the more I think about, the more such a frightening scenario makes sense to me and before I know it, I'm putting my shoes back on and creeping to the door. When I open it, I can see the light on under Cameron's bedroom door, so I know he's still awake, but as long as I'm quiet, I should be able to get out of here without him noticing that I'm gone. He'll only try and talk me out of what I'm planning on doing and I couldn't really blame him for trying, but I'd rather not give him that chance.

Closing my bedroom door behind me so it looks like I'm still in there if Cameron leaves his room at any point tonight, I tip-toe to the stairs and descend as slowly and quietly as I can. Then I creep into the kitchen and remove a pair of scissors from a drawer before I make it to the front door without any creaky floorboards giving me away. All I have to do then is turn the key in the lock before stepping outside.

I walk briskly to my destination with the scissors in hand, feeling the chill of being outside after dark in winter, but by the time I reach the couple's house again, I am warmed from the exercise. I see lights on inside the house, the same house I caused such a scene at earlier, and I creep closer, approaching one of the windows that has a net curtain hanging over it.

Carefully, I peer inside and look into the home and when I do, I see the male homeowner packing up a bag. He's wearing shorts and a t-shirt, and when I see him grab a tennis racket, I'm guessing he's getting ready to go and play a game. When I see him kiss his wife, the woman wearing the dressing gown and towel over her wet hair, it's clear he is leaving, so I quickly hide before he departs.

Crouching down behind a hedge, I hear the front door open, before the man closes it and walks to his car, his bag and tennis racket in tow. Then he jumps in behind the wheel and off he goes, clearly not too distressed after today's events to deviate from his exercise regime. Looking back at the window, I see the woman sitting on the sofa watching television and tucking into a box of chocolates.

I'm guessing he's the healthy one in the relationship.

With him out and her occupied, I seize my opportunity and go to the door, before trying the handle. It's unlocked, and I step into the spacious hallway, noting the pram by the foot of the stairs as well as the basket of child's clothes on the floor that is waiting to be taken up.

I assume the child is sleeping upstairs in her crib, so I go for the staircase, listening out for the woman making a move, but all I hear is the television and the occasional rustling in the chocolate box. Climbing the stairs, I can hardly believe I'm doing this, but if I want to find out for certain if this child is Tuppence or not, I have no choice. The police clearly aren't going to look into this any further for me, so I have to take matters into my own hands.

I see five doors up here but only one of them is closed, so I guess that might be the one behind which the little girl is sleeping, and sure enough, I'm right. As I enter, I hear a white noise machine playing and see a red light glowing in the corner of the room, which gives me just enough light to see the crib in the other corner. I step towards it and once I'm standing over it, I look down at the sleeping child inside.

I study her face – her closed eyes, her tiny nostrils, her little lips and her perfect ears, and I try to figure out if this is what my daughter looks like now. I study every single little feature of hers in the limited light there is in here, but the fact is that I have not seen her for a year, and she may have changed enough to make her no longer recognisable to me. This girl has thick curls of dark hair now, while Tuppence only had a few wispy tufts when she went missing, plus she's obviously grown a lot, so it's not as if I should be able to easily see my little girl in her appearance. I'll need something more accurate than my eyes.

Like a DNA test.

Reaching down into the crib and crossing whatever the last threshold of human decency is if I'm wrong about this, I carefully take hold of one of the little girl's hairs and use the scissors to cut it off her head. I'm worried she might wake up as I collect the hair sample, but she doesn't, and now I have what I came for, I can leave. But I linger by the crib for another moment, staring at the softly snoring child and wondering if I'm about to be reunited with my baby. If this is Tuppence, I just want to take her now, but there's no way I could get away with that. I have to do this the right way, a way Detective Jacobs would not be able to get me in trouble for, or at least not so much trouble that I couldn't get out of it quickly enough.

I leave the crib and the bedroom and head back down the stairs when I'm confident that the woman isn't lurking down there in the hallway. But she's still eating her chocolate, the rustle of wrappers music to my ears as I approach the door.

When I step outside, the street beyond is quiet, almost as quiet as it was on the night Tuppence was taken. With what I have in my possession now, I wonder if this is the start of me getting her back.

26

I made it back to bed without Cameron noticing that I had gone, and as he served me up yet another breakfast bagel in the morning, I asked him if it was okay if I ordered a couple of things to his house. Nothing major, just a few female toiletry necessities. He said yes, not needing or wanting to ask for any more details, which I knew would be the case, and that's all the groundwork I had to put in place for me to receive a package at his home that wouldn't arouse any suspicion.

The home DNA testing kit that I purchased online arrived at Cameron's house less than twenty-four hours after I snuck into that couple's house and plucked a hair from the head of the child sleeping in their home. Thanks to the speed of modern day delivery companies, I had the test quickly, and all I had to do then was use that stolen hair, along with one of Tuppence's. I already had several of them after finding them all over her remaining baby clothes in the days after her disappearance. Putting the two hairs inside the case, I then sent back the testing kit so people far cleverer than me could check the two samples and determine whether or not they were a match.

Patience has never been a virtue of mine, but I was going to have to wait at least forty-eight hours for the results, so I knew I'd have to keep myself occupied during that time. The first thing I had to do was deal with my mum, who had been calling and texting me and wondering where I was. She'd clearly realised I wasn't at home like I should be.

'I've just gone away with a friend for a couple of days,' I say in my message back to her, hoping she'll leave it at that. But this is my mother we're talking about, so there was little chance of that.

'A friend? Would this be a male friend?'

'No, Mother, I'm not dating.'

'Oh, okay. Where have you gone?'

'Just out of the city for a break.'

'You're not in Stirling, are you?'

'No, of course not.'

'Good. I know you were making the appeal on the anniversary, but you promised you wouldn't stay there.'

'I'm not in Stirling. Don't worry.'

Thankfully, Mum leaves her prying there, and I leave my phone in the bedroom before going downstairs to see what Cameron is up to. I find him sat at his dining room table with a laptop open in front him and several pieces of paper scattered around beside that. It looks like he's hard at work, or at least trying to be. But the sight of several scrunched up pieces of paper littering the floor around his chair suggests it might not be going as well as he'd hoped.

'Writing?' I ask him, lingering in the doorway and not wanting to go further into the room in case I disrupt him too much.

'Trying,' he replies with a weary sigh. 'But the creative juices just aren't flowing today.'

'I'm sure they will,' I say with a friendly smile. 'Just stick at it.'

'What are you doing today?' Cameron asks me then, sitting back in his chair and removing his hands from the keyboard.

'Not much,' I reply, which is true, although he has no idea there is a secretive DNA test currently underway. 'I might hang out here for a while, if that's okay, and then maybe go out for lunch.'

'Sounds good. You're more than welcome to relax here,' Cameron says cheerily, and I thank him before making myself a cup of tea and taking a seat on his sofa.

As I hear him tapping away at the keys in the other room, I decide to pick up one of his books again and take a proper look. They say you should never judge a book by its cover, so the only way to form a proper opinion is to actually open it up and read a few of the pages. So that's what I do, although once I have, it doesn't take me long to realise why Cameron is more of a struggling writer than a successful one. It's not that his writing is bad, it's just that his story isn't particularly exciting, and even though I make it through a couple of chapters, I'm hardly gripped. He has a plot line about a man murdering his wife using poison and the detective trying to catch him. But the detective character isn't compelling, and there are no twists. I feel bad for putting the book down in the end and when I do, I hope that whatever he is working on now is a little more interesting, for his sake as much as his readers.

Finishing my tea, I put my coat on and say goodbye to Cameron before walking into the city centre, and I spend a pleasant hour pottering around a few shops, though I don't buy anything because I can't be frivolous with money. Now I'm single, I don't have the benefit of another person's income to top me up if I spend too much of mine. I wonder how Leon is getting on with his own singledom these days. Maybe he's managing just fine. Or maybe he's already found somebody else to pair up with.

I don't know because Leon hasn't been very active on social media since we split. Nor have I, to be fair. Our days of fooling the world with smiling selfies and witty captions are over.

I'm planning on getting a bite to eat before heading back to Cameron's when I suddenly hear something amongst the hustle and bustle of the pedestrian-filled street that makes me freeze and my blood turn cold.

It's a woman's voice calling out to somebody.

And it sounds just like the woman I heard calling for help on the night Tuppence was taken.

'Hey! I'm over here!'

I turn to the sound of the woman's voice, but I can't find exactly who it is amongst the sea of people wandering this busy street. But it sounded so like that voice I heard before that I feel as if I'm very close to the woman who took my baby.

Is it the woman whose house I snuck into last night? Is she here somewhere? If so, it will only be further proof that she really is the culprit.

And then I see her, the woman who is calling out to her friend to get her attention.

But it's not who I thought it might be.

It's not the woman from last night.

It's Raquel.

I see one of my prime suspects cutting across the road with a pram, her child sitting inside it and giggling as she is rushed towards another woman on the other side of the street. This must be her friend, the woman Raquel was just calling out to, and when they're together, I see them hug, clearly old pals enjoying being back with each other once more.

I keep watching as Raquel and her friend chat for a moment before they enter a restaurant, and catching a few glimpses of them through the window, I see them being seated by a waitress. They're clearly out for lunch together and that tells me one thing.

Raquel is occupied for the foreseeable future.

That means no chance of her coming home early again and catching me trying to find out what is in her basement.

With the sound of her voice still rattling around in my head, a sound so similar to the one I heard before, I forget all about the couple and the DNA test and return my convictions to Raquel and what she might be hiding in that basement of hers.

Not wasting a second, I head for Buckingham Place, running as fast as I can until I reach the dreaded street, totally out of breath but aware that Raquel probably won't have even ordered her meal yet. Then I rush to her house, through the side gate, retrieving the key from under the garden furniture and then unlocking the back door and stepping inside.

The house is totally silent, but I soon start making noise as I look everywhere for the key to the locked basement door. I'm opening and closing cupboards, rummaging through drawers and turning all sorts of items upside down to see if there might be a key hidden somewhere, but I don't find one. Having extensively searched in the kitchen, living room and dining room, that only leaves the playroom down here, so I go into there, hoping I might get lucky.

As it was the last time I was here, there are toys scattered everywhere, and I quickly start rummaging through a toy chest full of them, to no avail. Then I see a fake kitchen set, the type a little boy or girl might have when they want to pretend that they are grown-up like their mummy and daddy and can cook a meal with their plastic pots and pans and fake food. I'm not expecting to find anything as I open the cupboards and drawers on the fake kitchen, but I have to look everywhere, although again, I have no luck. I'm getting very desperate, especially because I have no idea what stage Raquel is up to with her meal or when she'll be back.

Then I feel something underfoot.

Looking down, I realise I have trodden on something hard and bumpy, though I can't see what it is. That's because whatever it is is underneath the rug in this playroom.

Quickly stepping off it and lifting it up, I see exactly what I have been looking for.

A key, hidden underneath the rug.

This has to be it, I think as I scoop it up and run to the basement before trying it in the lock.

Please be it, I think as I turn the key.

And it is.

The door opens with a slight creak, and I peer inside, only to see darkness. I feel around on the wall for a light but can't locate one, so I guess I'm going to have to step into the dark if I'm to find one.

'Hello?' I call out, quietly at first but louder a second time. Then I say the name that's always on my mind.

'Tuppence?'

I listen out but no sounds come back at me. Is this stupid? Is this just an empty basement? Or does it hold a terrible secret?

Stepping in, I feel a wooden step beneath my feet, and as my eyes adjust slightly, I see more steps going down. There is a thin rail on the right, so I hold onto it as I descend carefully, and as I reach the bottom, I feel again on the wall for a light.

I find one this time and flick the switch and when I do, a bulb hanging from the centre of the basement flickers slowly to life. It takes a couple more flickers before it stays on and once it has, I can fully get a sense of my surroundings.

The first thing I see is a pram, folded down and sitting in the corner. Next to that is a bag full of baby clothes and beside that are a few toys. But it's the cot I'm drawn to in the other corner, and I rush towards it in case Tuppence is in there, though she is not. *But has she been?*

Looking around, I see more baby belongings, but it's the stack of newspapers that catch my eye, particularly when I see what is on the front cover of the paper on top.

It's a photo of me.

Picking up the newspaper, I recognise the photo and the headline. It was one of many stories that were printed about me and my search for my child, and as I rummage through the rest of the newspapers, I find more front cover exclusives about the case of the missing baby. So many articles were written about my daughter's disappearance and all of them seem to be here, not exactly catalogued but collected, nonetheless. Why? What need does Raquel have for keeping these? Unless she is guilty and this is some sort of sick stash of souvenirs.

Has Tuppence been in here? Is this where she was hidden when she was first taken so the police couldn't find her? If she was, where is she now?

I don't have any more time to keep searching around in this basement because I hear the creak of a floorboard above my head.

A second later and I see the door closing at the top of the stairs.

Then I hear the sound of the key turning in the lock.

27

A mixture of panic and calm comes over me in an instant - panic because I know I've just been locked in this basement, but calm because it seems to confirm to me that I am in the right place after all.

If Raquel didn't take my baby, why would she just lock me in here?

Racing up the stairs, I reach the door and try the handle, though it obviously doesn't move.

'Open this door!' I cry as I begin hitting it, desperate to be let out of a room that I willingly entered of my own accord, but that was before I knew somebody was lurking out there to trap me in here.

Raquel must have come back early from her meal. Did she see me? Did I inadvertently trigger a silent alarm that told her someone was in her home? Does she have cameras somewhere? Whatever has happened, I've been caught, and there is seemingly no way out.

'Raquel! Open this door! I know it's you out there!' I call out, hitting the door again several times and giving it a strong kick for good measure, not that it does anything. 'You can't get away with this! People know I'm here! They'll look for me and they'll get me out and then you'll be in trouble!'

None of that is true, but my captor doesn't need to know that as I hit the door again and again, but to no avail.

Why isn't she talking back to me? She could at least say something like she has caught me or that the police are on their way or anything that would at least let me know that she is listening to me in here. But there is nothing coming back from the other side of this door - no words, no desperate cries like mine, no revelling in victory, nothing.

So what does she plan to do to me now she has me?

My panic increases when I worry that she might just leave me in here. What if this door never opens? Nobody knows where I am. I didn't tell Cameron I was coming here, and Mum has no idea that I'm still in Stirling. Raquel could just keep this door locked and I'd be screwed, no way of escape and no way to call for help.

My phone!

I reach into my pocket and pull my mobile out in the hopes of making a call but alas, I have no signal. I suppose Raquel already knew that would be the case. Damn her, she's always one step ahead of me. But then I tell myself that eventually, when I do get reported missing, the police might be able to track my phone and if they do, they will hopefully see that this is the last location it was at. Then it won't take long for them to come to this house and kick down this door, although I'm not sure what they will find by then.

Me alive.

Or me dead?

'You took my baby!' I scream at the top of my lungs, afraid not just for myself but for Tuppence, who must have ended up in this same basement herself back when she was stolen from me. But where is she now if only I am in here? I don't know, but Raquel's actions in locking this door couldn't have made her look any more guilty, and I'm just cursing myself for getting distracted with other suspects when I knew deep down all along that this woman was the one behind the kidnapping.

'You think my baby can replace yours?' I call out. 'Well, she can't! She'll never be yours, no matter what you do and how much time goes by! She'll always be mine, and you'll always be a child snatcher! That's all you'll ever be! Is that how you want to be remembered? Because it's what's going to happen!'

It's disconcerting not to get any response to my anguished cries, and I can only imagine what Raquel is thinking and doing on the other side of this door. But, after at least ten more minutes of me demanding to be released and making all sorts of offensive declarations about my captor, Raquel goes and does the last thing I actually expected her to do.

She unlocks the door.

At least I presume she was the one who unlocked it, and after hearing the key turn in the lock, I don't waste my chance and try the handle, relieved when it lowers and the door opens, allowing me to run out...*into the clutches of a waiting police officer.*

'You're under arrest for breaking and entering and trespassing on private property,' comes the stern statement from the arresting officer, and he is quickly backed up by a colleague, the flash of the handcuffs as fleeting as the moment I thought my ordeal was about to be over.

'What's happening? I've just been locked in there! Where's Raquel? Where's the woman who has my baby?'

My questions do little to slow down the work of the police officers and as they try to lead me towards the front door, I strain my neck to get a glimpse of Raquel, though she's nowhere to be seen. It's only when we're outside the house that I see other people, most of them neighbours who have ventured out onto their doorsteps to see what is happening on their street this time. When they see me being led out of Raquel's house, the expressions on their face seem to say what they are thinking.

Not her again.

But there's still no sign of Raquel, which is very confusing because if she had called the police, why wouldn't she want to be out here witnessing their arresting of me? However, while she's not here, there is someone standing on her driveway as I am led to the waiting police car. It's a man in his early forties, and he is standing with his arms crossed as he watches me go. I don't recognise him but as I'm marched past him, I hear him thank the officers for their speedy assistance.

Wait, did this guy call the police?

Who the hell is he?

I don't know, and I'm bundled into the back of the police car before I have time to ask before being driven away from the street that is quickly becoming a regular scene for me to make headlines. I am wondering, or dreading, what the journalists in this city will write about me once they find out I've just been arrested for breaking into a home, but first, I have more pressing problems to deal with.

Detective Jacobs wants to know what I thought I was doing.

'I was trying to find my daughter. You should try and do the same, sometime,' I reply viciously, trying to put this back on him, though it's futile because I know I've committed a crime and I still have to answer for it, regardless of my desperate circumstances.

'I don't know what to say,' Jacobs replies wearily. 'I don't know what to say if that couple whose home you broke into choose to press charges because there's nothing I can do to help you. Losing your daughter doesn't give you the right to break into people's houses.'

'Wait, couple? What couple? I thought it was just Raquel who lives there?'

Jacobs frowns. 'Raquel's husband is the one who called us when you were locked in his basement.'

'Raquel's husband?'

I had no idea she was married and there was a man in that house because I'd never seen him before. Where the hell had he been hiding?

'Yes, he was working in his office in the loft when he heard you in his home. He came downstairs to investigate and when he realised where you were, he locked the door and called the police. He was quite distressed on the phone, as you might imagine a person would be if they had been working from home and heard somebody wandering around in their house.'

He was working in the loft? I didn't know he was there, but he clearly knew I was. All that time I thought I was being clever, waiting until Raquel was preoccupied before sneaking into her house, yet there was somebody in there with me the whole time?

But if I didn't know he was there, what else could that house be hiding?

'They're guilty,' I say defiantly. 'They took Tuppence. They're sneaky, can't you see that? Why would he lock me in if they were innocent?'

'Because he was scared! He had no idea who was in his house and what they wanted,' Jacobs tells me wearily. 'It could have been a very dangerous situation.'

'Yeah, for me and my daughter, not for him and his wife!' I cry. 'Ask him why he has newspaper articles about my daughter's disappearance in his basement! Explain that!'

'He's a journalist with a Scottish newspaper. I expect he has a lot of newspapers in his house. He's probably written some articles about your daughter himself. That doesn't mean he or his wife have taken her.'

I try to think of a comeback to that, but Jacobs doesn't want to hear it even if I had one.

'This has to stop,' he tells me, fixing me with a serious stare. 'I mean it, Gabby. You're just making things worse for yourself, and I'm worried for you. I'm worried about where it will end, and there's only so much I can do to help you.'

'Help me? When have you ever helped me? My daughter is still missing, in case you hadn't realised.'

'I've been helping you more than you know,' Jacobs says, and I can tell that he thinks he means it. 'I'm helping you right now because after this conversation, I will go and speak to the couple who currently want you charged, and I will try to persuade them that you made a mistake, due to your fragile situation, and that it won't happen again. If I'm successful, maybe I can keep you out of prison, though I can't promise it because it's their right to have you pay for what you did to them.'

'And what about what they did to me?' I cry. 'I was falsely imprisoned! And they took my child!'

Jacobs rubs his forehead, looking utterly exhausted at having to deal with me, before he tells me to wait here while he goes and speaks to Raquel and her partner. But just before he goes, I make sure to tell him what the first thing is that he should say to them.

He should say that I know they took my baby and if they think this is over, they are sadly mistaken.

28

Jacobs did as he said he would and spoke to Raquel and her husband, although I'm not sure if he told them what I wanted to say to them. He did, however, tell me the result of their conversation, laying out the facts of it very clearly for me so there could be no confusion on my part.

That couple were sick and tired of me interfering in their lives, as was everybody else in and around Buckingham Place, and while they were aware they could have me punished for entering their home illegally, they were willing to let me go.

But only on one very clear condition.

I leave Stirling and never come back to bother them or their neighbours ever again.

I scoffed at the proposal that the detective put forward to me when I first heard it, dismissing the notion of never coming back to the city where my daughter was last seen, as well as simply giving up the idea that I might ever be able to find her here again one day. But Jacobs took his time in spelling out to me just what I was facing if I didn't agree to the offer, and it was sobering to say the least.

The evidence against me was solid. Having been caught on private premises in what was clearly a pre-mediated decision to enter the home of another person without permission, I could be facing a custodial sentence of six months, perhaps longer, depending on who presided over the case and how strict they turned out to be at upholding the law. At best, I was looking at a sizeable fine and community service, but if I was to reject the idea of leaving Stirling for good, Raquel and her partner would press for a prison sentence and would most likely get it if they made a show of telling the judge how much pain and distress my breaking into their home had caused them. I was already looking at a restraining order which would forbid me from coming within two hundred yards of Raquel's home, which would be a criminal act to breach, but Jacobs didn't even want me to risk that and just kept making his main point again and again until I started to understand my situation.

Accept that I have to leave Stirling and the poor residents of Buckingham Place alone forever – *or have my life ruined even more by adding in a criminal record to go with me being a grieving mother and ex-wife.*

It took a lot longer for Jacobs to make me see sense, but the fact I'm currently in a car on the way to Stirling train station shows what course of action I have ultimately decided to take. The detective is right, loath as I am to admit it, and it's surely better for me to leave than face prison. But the real tipping point in my decision-making process came when I received an email from the company who supplied me with the DNA testing kit. The results were in, and as I opened the email, my heart was thumping as I wondered if it was going to be the moment when I received conclusive proof that my daughter was now in the hands of somebody else. But it was not. The DNA test confirmed there was no match between that couple's child and my missing one and with that, another suspect was ruled out, along with just about the only hope I had of making a breakthrough in the mysterious and heart-wrenching case.

'What time is your train again?' the man sitting in the driver's seat beside me asks, and I turn to Cameron and remind him that my train is due to depart Stirling at eleven o'clock.

'Ahh, loads of time,' he says with a smile, but he quickly covers it up when he realises that I'm far from happy about what I have planned today. Soon, as I assured Detective Jacobs, who in turn would have assured Raquel and her husband, I will leave this city. I'll be back in Edinburgh within the hour, back to Mum's place, back to my old job, back to my miserable life. If it wasn't for the fact that I still harbour hopes of one day seeing my daughter again, I'd give some consideration to jumping in front of the next train rather than getting on it but no, I'd never do that. Not while there is still hope, although that hope is fading as quickly as the passengers file in and out of the station as we reach it.

After Cameron parks up, I gather up my few belongings, and as we make our way inside the station, I look around, half expecting to see Raquel and her baby watching me go, or Jacobs standing somewhere, sipping a coffee and making sure I'm doing as I promised. But I don't see anybody I recognise, only Cameron walking alongside me, his shoulders hunched and head bowed, as if he knows this is hard for me and he's wanting to show he's struggling a little with it too.

'Thank you for all your help,' I say to him as we reach the ticket barriers where only I have a pass to get any further. 'I really appreciate all you have done for me and know that you didn't have to do any of it. You've been incredibly kind to me, and I'll never forget that.'

'It's been no trouble,' Cameron says before rethinking that statement slightly. 'Okay, so maybe it has been a little trouble, but I totally understand why. I think you're incredibly brave, as well as incredibly loyal to your daughter, and you've only done what any mother would do. I'm just sorry this story hasn't had the happy ending it deserves, but hopefully, one day it will.'

I hug Cameron then before I start crying and as we separate, I thank him one more time.

'If you really want to show your appreciation, just buy one of my books,' he jests. 'Lord knows there's plenty of them still out there unsold.'

I can't help but laugh at that before wishing him all the best with his career and with life in general. But while this feels like a permanent goodbye, I try to end this on a positive note by telling him that I'll see him one day.

'I'll bring Tuppence to meet you once I have her back,' I say, which might make me sound incredibly delusional, but so what?

Thankfully, like the lovely man that he is, Cameron humours me rather than giving me a harsh dose of reality and says he would like that very much, before he wishes me well and I turn to hand my ticket to the inspector manning the barriers.

After passing through without issue, I turn and give Cameron one last wave and he waves back before I make my way out onto the platform. I note Cameron looked a little lonely as he bid me farewell, and I expect he'll miss having company in his house again. Hopefully, he'll find someone to fill that void in his life soon. I think it's safe to say he'll find it far quicker than I will.

I walk past a couple of passengers with large suitcases and take a seat on a bench before looking up at the screen above the platform to check that my train is still on time. It is, and it's now only eight minutes to go until I leave this fateful place forever. I'm so lost in my thoughts that I fail to notice that a fellow passenger is approaching me and it's only when they sit down beside me and say my name that I realise I have captured somebody's attention.

'Excuse me?' I say as I turn to look at the man beside me, and when I see him, he seems vaguely familiar, though I can't quite place him. The curly hair, the scruffy clothing, the stubble on his chin and the way he leans in slightly towards me as he goes to speak to me is all recognisable. Then he tells me how we know each other.

'Do you remember me? We were chatting in the pub the other night. I almost took you home and treated you like a gentleman should, but we were rudely interrupted.'

Oh God, that's how I know this guy. He's the man who Cameron saved me from, the one I would have been making a big mistake going home with if only that friendly writer hadn't intervened. Ralph, I think his name is.

'Erm, hi,' I say, feeling awkward and cursing my bad luck for running into this guy.

What does he think is going to happen? We'll just pick up where we left off and I'll be at his house within the next ten minutes?

'You know, you hurt my feelings the other night,' Ralph says with a chuckle whilst eyeing me up and down, not that there's much to see because I'm wearing a thick coat. 'But I can forgive you for that. It's Cameron I blame. He's the one who spoilt our fun.'

He obviously knows Cameron and remembers how he kept me away from making a mistake while heavily intoxicated, but I just smile politely and try not to make a big deal about it.

'Cameron is a friend of mine,' I say. 'He was just worried about me as I'd had a lot to drink.'

'A friend?' my uninvited guest on this bench scoffs. 'Is that what you think he is? A friend? You clearly don't know the real Cameron.'

'What's that supposed to mean?'

'Don't look at me like I'm the weird one,' Ralph says sternly. 'You're the one who trusts a crime writer. Tell me, is it a coincidence that a guy who spends all day writing about husbands and wives that kill each other suddenly ends up with a dead wife himself and pretends like he didn't have anything to do with it?'

'What are you talking about? Cameron's wife was ill,' I say, recalling what Cameron told me about his partner's passing.

'Oh right, of course she was,' comes the sniggering response. 'If you believe that, you'll believe anything.'

Ralph gets up to go then, but he can't just say something like that and leave it, so I ask him what he is talking about. That's when he turns back to me and says something that sends a shiver down my spine, even with this bulky coat on.

'I bet he told you that I was dangerous and worth staying away from,' Ralph says with a shake of the head. 'But I'm telling you now – Cameron is the dangerous one. Believe me, you'd have been far safer with me than with him.'

The man leans in then and looks me dead in the eyes before saying something that is only in earshot of me and no one else on this platform.

'I know who you are and why you're here. You're looking for your daughter and you think somebody in Stirling has a secret that involves her. Well, let me tell you something. If there's one person in Stirling with secrets, it's Cameron Cargill.'

With that, the man just laughs again before shuffling away, and I'm left alone on the bench wondering what just happened. I'm only interrupted when I hear the announcer letting everyone on the platform know that the train to Edinburgh is now approaching. But as I see the line of linked carriages moving down the track towards me, I suddenly change my plans.

I'm not leaving Stirling.

Not now I know the person who has supposedly been helping me might just turn out to be the biggest liar of them all.

29

'Gabby? What are you doing here? I thought you'd be on the train by now!'

Cameron is shocked to see me on his doorstep but not as shocked as he'll be when I tell him about my little conversation on the platform that involved him and his past.

'You've been lying to me,' I say, pointing a finger at him. 'I thought I could trust you! I thought you were the one person in this city who was on my side!'

Cameron's surprise at my appearance is matched by his surprise at my outburst, but still, despite what I've said, he pretends to have my best interests at heart.

'You're supposed to be on the way back to Edinburgh. What if somebody sees you? You'll be arrested!' he says, but I brush off his 'concerns' because I simply no longer believe he is genuine anymore.

'Why did you lie to me? Why did you pretend like you were looking out for me? All I wanted was somebody to tell me the truth here, anybody, but you're just another liar!'

Cameron looks over my shoulder then, and he must see one of his neighbours watching us because he advises me to come inside so we can talk in private. But I refuse to set foot in his house again until he has told me the truth.

'You lied about your wife. You said she was ill, but everyone here thinks you hurt her. Did you?'

'No, of course not!'

'Tell me the truth! I thought you had helped me that night we met, and now I'm not so sure. What else are you hiding? Do you know something about my child? Are you saving it for a book? Did you think you'd just befriend me and get some insight into what life has been like for me as research for one of your characters?'

'Of course not! You're being ridiculous.'

'Am I? I don't know what to believe anymore.'

I turn away then, angry and fed up, but not just at Cameron. At everyone. At life. What's the point of even trying anymore?

'She killed herself.'

I freeze when I hear Cameron's words behind me, and when I turn back, I see him looking down at his feet, avoiding eye contact with me.

'My wife. She took her own life. I just told you she was ill because I'm ashamed of what really happened.'

I can see that shame written all over Cameron's face, and it's impossible to carry on being mad at him when he looks like he does.

'She'd always been a big drinker, but it got heavier as her job got more stressful. I tried to get her help, but she didn't stop, even when she told me she had. Then she lost her job, and with my books not doing well, we didn't have much money. That made her more stressed and…'

Cameron's voice trails off, but I can guess the ending to that sentence.

'I've blamed myself for what she did every day since,' he says. 'I woke up one morning to find she had overdosed on sleeping tablets and vodka, but I never should have gone to bed that night. We'd argued before and I stormed off, but if I'd stayed awake, if I'd tried to talk to her, maybe…'

Cameron shakes his head, but now I have the truth, it's difficult to be mad at him.

'The police and the paramedics were satisfied that she had meant to kill herself, but people in this city need a more exciting story than that to gossip about, so they made up tales of how I secretly planned it. As if just because I write about crime, I'm a criminal myself. But I'm not, I'm just a guy who lost his wife.'

A tear runs down his cheek then, and the only thing I can think to do is give him a hug. After he has apologised again for lying to me, I feel like making an apology of my own.

'I'm sorry I accused you of keeping secrets from me. About Tuppence. That was stupid.'

'It's okay. I lied, so I guess you didn't trust me. But honestly, when I met you in that pub that first night, I was trying to help you.'

'I know,' I say with a nod of my head.

We linger on the doorstep for a few more moments, and when I look around the street, I see one of the neighbours at their window, clearly watching us, although they try to pretend that they're not when they see me looking.

'So, what's your plan? Please tell me you're still leaving,' Cameron says. 'I'd hate for you to get in trouble just because you came back to talk to me.'

'I am leaving,' I say, surprised I even got so worked up that I came back here in the first place, but I guess the red mist descended back on that platform.

'I'm sorry about your wife, Cameron,' I say as I turn away. 'Goodbye.'

'Goodbye, Gabby,' Cameron replies. 'I'm sorry about your daughter.'

With that, we part again, and though I've missed my original train when I return to the station, I buy a ticket for the next one, and this time, there are no unexpected interruptions.

As Stirling shrinks into the distance, I look away from the train window, and as my carriage rumbles along the tracks, I try to tell myself that I won't end up like Cameron, who is clearly full of regret and shame. But by the time my train has reached its destination, I know I'm cursed to suffer the same fate as him forever.

Two people who feel like they neglected a loved one for just a moment and never got the chance to make up for it again.

I wish him all the best.

At least he has his writing to focus on.

I guess I'll have to find something to keep me busy too.

ONE YEAR LATER

30

'Thank you for shopping here. Have a good day.'

I smile at the young woman who has just purchased two books and a small lamp and watch her leave the shop before I go back to what was keeping me busy before she walked in, namely organising the large collection of DVDs that were kindly donated to us today. Feeling the contentment that comes with volunteering in a charity shop every Saturday, I work quietly and easily, my mind and hands occupied, which I've found has been the best way for me to cope with my past.

Twelve months on since I last set foot in Stirling, I've kept myself busy through a variety of ways, all with the aim of not dwelling too much on Tuppence and what might have befallen her. I still have my office job that takes up forty hours of my weekdays, and several gym classes keep me engaged on the weeknights. Each Saturday is spent here, working alongside a couple of other volunteers as we sell all sorts of items to all sorts of people in the pursuit of raising much needed funds for worthy causes. Sundays are always the hardest day, but between seeing Mum, attending a gym class and cleaning every inch of my flat, I tend to get through it before another busy week begins.

That's how my last year has panned out. I'm fitter than I was, both mentally and physically, and while it might not be the healthiest thing to keep myself so busy to the point where I barely have a moment alone, it's doing the job of keeping me functioning.

'How are you getting on with those DVDs?' asks Carol, a fellow volunteer with a warm smile, as she passes by, carrying a wooden chair that she plants down in front of the window before going in search of a price tag.

'I'm trying to alphabetize them, but it could take me a while,' I admit before Carol bats the air.

'Oh, don't bother doing that. Just stack them up and put them on a shelf. The customers will find what they're looking for if we have it.'

I take that advice and carry the DVDs to the nearest vacant shelf before finding a sticker and writing ***ALL DVDs - £1*** on it. With that simple job done, I check the time and see that it's already midday, which means only one thing.

'I'm going for my lunch. Do you want anything?' I ask Carol as I pick up my handbag and coat and head for the door, but she tells me she's fine, so I walk out onto the street with nobody's food to buy but my own.

Wandering along the row of shops that make up this side of the main road, I casually glance through the windows of several of them, more out of habit than anything else. But as I pass the large bookstore just before I get to the bakery, I stop in my tracks when I see the book that is most prominently on display inside.

Having walked past here many times, I'm aware that there is always a *'Book Of The Week'* showcased to tempt in book lovers as they walk by. But it's not so much that I'm tempted by this particular book, more shocked, because I recognise the name of the author.

Cameron Cargill.

It has to be the author I befriended in Stirling, right? How many authors with that name can there be? Plus, he writes crime thrillers, and the front cover of this book certainly fits that genre with the title *The Missing Child* and an image of a shadowy figure pursuing the silhouette of a youngster down a dark street.

Entering the bookshop, I discover a whole section of a shelf dedicated to Cameron's latest book, and I pick up the first paperback I can and thumb through to the author bio page. Sure enough, there is a photo of Cameron's face smiling back at me, as well as a brief description of his life and writing career.

From Stirling.

His fifth published book.

A real literary talent.

Those are just some of the phrases that jump out at me before I start flicking through the pages, impressed and curious because Cameron really seems to have done well for himself considering he was definitely more in the camp of 'struggling writer' the last time I saw him.

Deciding that, as his friend, I should support him, I take the book to the pay-point and purchase it from the woman, who tells me it is a "must read" when I hand it over to her. I tell her that I actually met the author once and she is thrilled by that before I leave the bookstore and enter the bakery. No sooner have I bought myself a sandwich, I find the nearest available bench on the street and take a seat before tucking into my lunch and beginning my new book, reading the back cover blurb first.

That's when I quickly realise what gave Cameron the inspiration for this sudden career boost of his.

The story is about a couple on holiday in Glasgow who lose their child and battle to find out the truth of what happened. It's obviously an idea taken straight from my experience, although at least Cameron had the decency to change the setting slightly. But just how much has my awful experience informed his story?

Flicking through the pages, I speed read, forgetting both about my sandwich and the fact that I only have a half-hour lunch break. I quickly get a grasp of the central characters – the wife who seems stressed and the husband who seems aloof – where might Cameron have got that from, I wonder? The central child in the story is a boy, so at least Cameron altered the gender of the missing youngster, but as I read about how they lose him whilst out shopping and frantically run around the city trying to find him again, it's blatantly obvious Cameron has drawn from real life to create his apparent masterpiece.

Am I mad at him? I don't know. Children go missing all over the world and parents have to deal with it; it's not as if I have ownership over that awful experience. But there are parts of this that are getting very close to replicating my story, especially when I get to the part where the police investigation surrounding the missing child starts to focus on one street in particular.

Cameron hasn't called the street 'Buckingham Place' but with the way he describes the luxurious homes and affluent residents inside them, it's easy for me to make the connection. But then, well past the end of my lunch break but totally gripped by the book, I read something that I don't recognise.

Cameron has written that one of the houses on the street was sold not long after the girl went missing and the seller is where the police should focus their efforts.

I wonder what made him think of that? It's an interesting plot twist, that a child went missing on a street and then the home was sold, as if the kidnappers wanted to get away from the scene of the crime as quickly as possible. I guess this is the part of the book where it veers more into fiction than fact, but I suppose Cameron had to be a lot more creative with the second part of his story seeing how my own one is so mysterious and unresolved. But as I turn another page, I'm wondering if Cameron really has been struck by inspiration or if he is, once again, just copying something that happened in real life.

Putting down the book and taking out my phone from my handbag, I go back to the website I used last year when I was snooping at the houses on Buckingham Place to see how much they were all worth. But I'm not looking for valuations now, rather if any of them have sold within the past twelve months or so.

I see several houses, including Raquel's, but all the sale dates for them are further in the past than the timeframe I'm searching for. And then I see it.

A house on Buckingham Place was sold eight months after my daughter disappeared.

That's the first sale on that street in years. People rarely move from there once they are in, but this person decided it was time for a change.

Who was it, or more importantly, which house?

As I'm wondering about Cameron and how he has clearly used further parts of reality to spice up his bestselling new book, I do some more digging on the internet until I lower my phone and put a hand to my mouth in horror.

I've now figured out which house it was that sold.

It's the house directly opposite where my daughter was taken.

31

I always felt it would have to take something special to see me return to Stirling. Maybe a possible sighting of my little girl that warranted looking into. A phone call from Detective Jacobs with a new lead, perhaps. But, as it turns out, it's a new discovery on my part that has led me back to this city and now I'm here, I'm wondering if I have just found out a way to breathe new life into the mystery of my daughter's disappearance.

After reading a large part of Cameron's new book and subsequently getting the idea to check the property listings online, I made my excuses at the charity shop to get out of the rest of my Saturday shift and boarded the first train I could get on to Stirling. Now I'm here, I'm rushing as quickly as I can to the estate agency who the internet tells me handled the most recent house sale on Buckingham Place and when I get there, I am hoping they can enlighten me as to who might have lived there and, most importantly, where they might be living now.

'No!' I cry when I see the *'Closed'* sign on the front door of the agency, and despite trying the handle and knocking on the glass, there is nobody inside to come and help me.

When I check the time, I see that it is after five o'clock, so I suppose it's understandable that they have finished for the day, and it is a weekend, but it doesn't help me at all. I try the phone number for the office, wondering if I might be able to get the manager, or at least an employee, who doesn't mind helping out somebody in need, but there is no answer, and I accept I'll have to wait to make any further progress here.

Almost.

Having hit one dead end, I decide to try another avenue and plan on having a conversation with Detective Jacobs, or at least one of his colleagues, at the station when I can get there. But that's on the other side of the city from where I am, and there is somebody a little nearer. So, after marching across several roads, I reach another door, one that I am more confident will be answered.

After banging on Cameron's door four times, I wait for the author to answer, wondering just how stunned he will be to see me back. He'll certainly have some explaining to do when I ask him about his new book and namely, why he failed to get in touch with me to let me know that somebody moved from Buckingham Place recently. If he deemed it worthy of noting in his fictious police investigation, surely it would have been worthy of him to mention it in a real-life one.

Frustratingly, there is no answer, though I keep banging on the door several more times to make sure. The noise I'm creating on this quiet street draws the attention of someone though – one of Cameron's next-door neighbours, and they come out to investigate.

'Can I help you?' a woman in her sixties asks as she pokes her head out from inside her own home.

'I need to speak to Cameron,' I say. 'Do you know if he's in?'

'Let me guess, you're a fan,' the woman says with a wry smile. 'That makes two of us. How wonderful is his new book? I've read it through twice and would read it a third time if I could, but I leant my copy to my sister.'

'I'm not a fan, I'm an old friend,' I say, before knocking again and assuming the neighbour can't be much help to me.

'Oh, I see. Well, you're not going to find him here,' she says, and that gets me to stop knocking.

'What?'

'Cameron moved out a few months ago. To a bigger place, I imagine. I'm sure all the royalties from *The Missing Child* means he's got somewhere much nicer than here. Can't say I blame him. I'd move too if I had the money, but never mind.'

'Do you know where he's gone?' I cry, hoping I get to give the newly minted author a piece of my mind about his latest scribblings.

'No, sorry. He didn't say, and I didn't pry. Although I do know where he is at six o'clock this evening.'

'You do?'

'Yes, he's at the Grand Hotel. He's doing a book signing there. I'd have been there myself, right at the front of that queue, if I hadn't promised that I'd look after my granddaughter tonight. She's asleep inside now. She's only four months old, bless her. They're so sweet at that age, aren't they?'

'Thank you,' I say as I rush away from the front door and the neighbour who bids me farewell.

My next stop is the hotel where Cameron is hosting his book signing, and as I reach the door, I see a couple of people going inside, a copy of the now-famous author's latest novel in their hands. But there are far more people inside, and as I see the long line stretching through one of the reception rooms in this hotel, I get a very visual sense of just how popular Cameron's writing has become.

I see the man of the hour sitting at a table at the back of the room, his head down and the pen in his hand moving across one of the pages of his book, the queue in front of him snaking all the way back towards me. But I don't plan to get in that queue and skip right past the line, instead approaching the table and ignoring the member of staff who tries to politely inform me that I am to wait my turn like everybody else.

'Cameron! We need to talk,' I say as I reach the table, and as the author looks up, the pen falls from his hand.

'Gabby? I wasn't expecting to see you here,' he says, looking sheepish rather than smug like he looked a minute ago.

'And I wasn't expecting you to write a book about me and my daughter to turn a profit, or to keep potentially vital information about what really happened from me!'

'Please, madam, you need to join the queue like everybody else,' the staff member tries, gently touching one of my arms to guide me back to where I should be. But I brush her off and step closer to Cameron and the stack of books beside him on the desk.

'Why didn't you tell me somebody sold their house on that street? What if they took my daughter? You thought it was good enough for your story but not good enough for me to hear about? Why? Because who cares about the poor mother who you clearly used to write such a compelling tale!'

I pick up one of the books then and launch it at the signage behind Cameron, the signage with a big photo of his face on, along with the title of his bestselling book.

'Someone call the police,' I hear the woman behind me say, but Cameron quickly gets up out of his seat, although that may just be because he's worried that I'm about to throw the next book I pick up at him.

'No! There's no need to call the police. I can handle this,' he says before he tells me to follow him to a side room where we can talk more privately.

I see plenty of puzzled faces from all the readers in the queue as I follow the flustered author into an empty room, and I wonder if any of them captured what just happened on their phones to upload to social media. That would certainly get people talking about Cameron's book, if there aren't enough people doing so already.

'I'm sorry,' Cameron starts with when we're alone. 'I can see how this looks bad and looks like I used you to sell a story, and the truth is that I did. I mean, I was trying to help you back when you stayed with me, but I also needed a new story, and you had such a compelling one. I shouldn't have used it, but I did, and now my career has taken off and I feel bad because I've clearly hurt you. How can I make it up to you?'

'Why didn't you tell me about the house that was sold?' I demand to know.

'I didn't think it was relevant.'

'How could it not be relevant? It's the house directly opposite where Tuppence was taken!'

'But it was sold several months after she went missing, not the day after. I presume the resident just wanted to change homes, nothing more to it. If I genuinely thought it had anything to do with your daughter, of course I would have told you and the police.'

'Yet you deemed it worthy of a plot point in your book, as if the person selling the house was involved in the kidnap.'

'Yes, but I write fiction!'

'Do you?'

I stare at Cameron, but as he looks back uselessly at me, I see he really is just an author who desperately needed an idea for a new book. That's why I just shake my head at him and walk away, ignoring his continued apologies as I leave him and the rest of his fans behind in the hotel to go back to enjoying their fictitious crimes. But I have a real one to solve, which is why my next stop is the police station.

32

I went straight from the book signing to the police station, though Detective Jacobs wasn't on duty when I got there. The best I got was Detective McAndrews, a stern-looking woman of fifty who had even less patience for me and my wild theories than her colleague used to have.

'You need to look into the person who sold that house,' I had tried several times. 'They might have moved because they're hiding something. Find them and question them!'

'If I'm not mistaken, a restraining order was filed against you by the residents of Buckingham Place,' McAndrews had reminded me. 'I can see why now with behaviour like this. People sell their homes and move all the time. It doesn't mean they are guilty of a crime, and certainly not one as serious as child abduction.'

I'd tried several more times to get the detective to at least look into the house move, but to no avail, and after the disappointing trip to the estate agents and the confrontation with Cameron at the hotel, I was left with little to show from my return to Stirling. That was until I decided to ignore McAndrews's advice that I leave Stirling soon before anyone who filed a restraining order against me sees me and invokes police action.

I ignored it by going straight back to Buckingham Place.

My destination was the house that had recently been sold and as I knocked on the door, I nervously looked around the dark street, wondering if any of the neighbours would peep outside and see me and call the police, fearing that the deluded, desperate mother was back to torment them all over again. But I didn't see any faces at the windows, nor any police sirens, only the face of the female homeowner I had just disturbed inside this house.

'Hello. Sorry to bother you. I was wondering if you could help me,' I begin politely, aware that this new resident won't know me quite as intimately as everyone else around here, so I can make a good first impression. 'I was wondering if you had an address for the person who sold you this house.'

'The person who sold me this house? Why do you ask?'

'Well, it's a little awkward, actually.'

I think about spinning a lie then but, ultimately, decide to just risk telling the truth, or at least a portion of it.

'You may have heard on the news last year about a baby girl being taken in Stirling,' I say. 'Well, she was actually taken right over there.'

I point across the dark street to the exact spot, which is not far at all from this front door I stand at.

'Oh my, I did hear about that,' the homeowner says sadly. 'It happened right here?'

I'm guessing both the seller and the estate agent failed to mention that. I wonder why?

'Yes, it happened here.'

'Oh my gosh. I'm so sorry, but I'm not sure how I can help.'

'I'm just trying to talk to the people who were around that day and see if anything can jog their memory,' I say. 'I know it's a long shot because quite a bit of time has passed, but I hope you understand that I can't stop looking for my daughter. Are you a mother?'

'Yes, I am. I have two sons.'

'Then you understand.'

'Of course!'

The woman looks heartbroken for me and clearly wants to help, but she doesn't look like she can.

'You say you need an address for where they moved to? I'm sorry, but I don't have that.'

'Do you have a name at least?' I ask in hope.

'Their name?'

The woman thinks about that.

'Yes, I do actually. I'll have it saved in my phone. I was texting the owner of this house a few times back when we were interested in buying. I had a few questions for her. Just things about the property. I might still have her name and number saved.'

The woman goes to get her phone then, and I wait patiently as she checks it, before she smiles.

'Yes, I have it here. Her name was Cara. Would you like her number? I'm sure she would understand me passing it on if it might be able to help you in some way.'

'Thank you, that's great,' I say as I use my phone to take the digits. 'Do you have a surname for her?'

'Erm,' the woman thinks before she calls out for someone called Ed.

A man appears then, presumably her husband, and after she has told him who I am and why I'm here, she asks if he can recall the surname of the previous owner.

'Brunswick,' he says, displaying a fantastic memory, and I thank him before typing that name into Facebook and bringing up a couple of results.

'Sorry, just so I can put a face to the name, do you recognise her from any of these photos?' I ask, and the couple lean in to look at the available options of 'Cara Brunswick's' on social media showing on my phone before Ed points at the third one down.

'That's her,' he says. 'Pleasant woman. She actually gave us a good deal on this place, didn't she, darling?'

'Yes,' she confirms. 'We were a little under the asking price, but she wanted a quick sale so took our second offer. We couldn't believe we got this house for what we did in the end. It really is a wonderful home. It's just so sad what happened here.'

Hearing that Cara seemed keen to sell and accepted a lower offer is interesting but not as much as the fact I now have her name and image to work on. As I look at the photo of the pretty brunette who used to live here, I don't recognise her from back when the neighbours were pouring out onto the street and the police were making their checks. She must have been around but if she was, she stayed out of my view.

'You say you don't know where she moved to?' I ask again, wondering if Ed's memory might have retained that golden nugget of information too.

'No, sorry,' they both say with a shake of the head before suggesting that the estate agent might be able to help me, unless that information is protected, which it probably is.

I thank the couple for their help and turn away, pondering how I am going to track down this Cara Brunswick to see if she moved away to hide something sinister. But before I reach the end of the driveway, I hear Ed's voice behind me telling me to wait a moment.

I turn back and do as he says as he disappears back into the house, and while I'm not sure what it is that I'm waiting for, I'm hoping it's something useful.

It is.

'This is the removals company who took Cara's things away when she left,' Ed tells me after he returns and produces a small business card that I approach him to take. 'The company posted this through our letterbox, so we found it when we moved in ourselves. I guess it's a good way of advertising.'

Ed hands me the card and I study it, seeing the logo for a removals van company beside the name of the company itself – ***Stirling Shifters.***

'I thought the name was quite funny,' Ed says before his wife rolls her eyes, but I'm not laughing, I'm just happy because this is a brilliant lead. This company must know where Cara went next if they removed her belongings from this house.

'Thank you so much,' I say. 'This is really helpful.'

With the card in my possession, I walk away, eager for tomorrow when I will be making a visit to this removals company in the hopes that I'll get the address I require. If I do, I know where I'll be going after that.

I'll be going to pay Cara a visit to find out exactly why she moved away from this street when every other homeowner around here seems so eager to stay.

33

I checked myself into a cheap motel in Stirling after leaving Buckingham Place, needing somewhere to lay my weary head down and get some rest before what I am hoping is going to be an eventful day today. Up bright and early, not just because I have things to do but because I haven't slept past dawn since Tuppence went missing, I check back out of the motel and get on my way.

I find the office for *Stirling Shifters* easily enough, following the directions on my phone until I get to a small office that looks like it could do with a fresh coat of paint and a new sign above the door. I see a large van parked outside with the company name printed across the side of it and when I enter the office, I find an overweight man in his fifties wearing a tight t-shirt emblazoned with the company logo. When he spots me walking in, he eyes me up and down before taking a sip from his coffee, a half-eaten bacon sandwich lying on top of a paper wrapper beside his keyboard on the desk.

'Morning, darling. How can I help?' he asks me in a gruff voice before wiping the corners of his mouth to remove a few of the breadcrumbs that were lingering there.

The office is cold and sparsely decorated, and I try to ignore the calendar on the wall that shows a topless woman lying on a beach as I make my way to this man's desk and prepare to ask for something he might not be willing to give me.

'Hi. You did the removals for an old friend of mine recently. Cara Brunswick. Do you remember?'

'The posh woman on Buckingham Place? Yeah, I remember her,' the man says with a nod. 'Very pretty lady. Almost as pretty as you.'

The man picks up his bacon sandwich and takes another bite, chewing it slowly as he watches me to see how his 'compliment' has landed. I think the best thing to do is just ignore that part of his answer and focus on the part where he said he remembered her.

'Great. I was wondering, could you tell me where you moved her belongings to?'

'You want her new address?'

'Yes, if possible.'

'Why?'

The man keeps chewing and staring, staring and chewing, and I realise he's enjoying holding the power in our interaction.

'Like I said, I'm an old friend of hers, but sadly, we've lost touch. I was hoping to go and see her again, but I don't have her new address.'

'If you're a friend, can't you just message her? You have a phone? Social media? This is the year 2024. Please tell me you don't still communicate via letters.'

The man seems amused at that and seems to be hoping that I'll find it funny too, so I pretend that I do, laughing falsely, just to keep him on side.

'No, of course not, don't be silly,' I say with a smile, which he seems to warm to. 'It's just that it's been a while since we've seen each other, and I was actually hoping to surprise her, if I can. You know, turn up at her new house with a bottle of wine and some chocolates. I think she'd like that.'

'I see,' the man says, leaning back in his seat and as he does, his t-shirt rides up a little around his waistline, exposing some of his bulging belly. I'm guessing that's not the first bacon sandwich he's had this year, or even this week.

'Now, suppose that I could help you,' he says, brushing off more crumbs, these ones on his clothes. 'What would be in it for me?'

'You'd get to do a good deed for a damsel in distress,' I say, hoping that will be enough, but I can already tell it won't be.

'The thing is, we're not supposed to give out the addresses of our customers. Just some silly company policy. But, in my capacity as one of the managers here, I like to make exceptions, in particular for people like you.'

I watch the man's eyes move up and down me again and take a deep breath, trying to stay calm in the presence of this pretty gross pervert.

'Let's say I could give you the address,' he goes on, his eyes lingering on my chest area even though it's wrapped beneath my coat and scarf. 'I'd like to have something in return.'

'What would that be?' I ask nervously, wondering if it's not too late for me to leave here and try my luck at the estate agents instead.

'I'd like you to go for a drink with me this evening after work. There's a pub I drink in most nights, and I think the other regulars there would be very impressed if they saw me walk in with you on my arm.'

'A drink? That's it?'

'Well, we'll start with one drink and see where the night takes us,' he goes on, grinning. 'I have to warn you, things can get pretty lively in that pub. It could turn into a bit of a late night. You might overindulge at the bar. You might need help getting home. Who knows? So, what do you say?'

Every cell in my body is screaming at me to say no and get away from this creep as quickly as possible. But he can give me Cara's address, and that's all I need, so I agree to the drink before asking for the address.

'You'll get that tonight after you meet me outside the pub,' I'm told, ruining any hope I had of just obtaining the address and then getting out of here quickly.

With our 'date' set, I leave the office and try my luck at the estate agents, hoping they'll be helpful without being sleazy, meaning I could just stand up the man I'm supposed to meet for a drink tonight. But as expected, they aren't willing to provide me with personal details of any of their clients. I do have Cara's phone number, so I consider calling her, but what would I say? The truth? That I think she sold her house and moved because she has my child and I want to know where she is right now? If she does have Tuppence, that would only spook her, and she could be on the move again and I'd never track her down, if so. That means my only hope, currently, is to go to the pub tonight and put up with an awkward situation for as long as it takes for me to get what I want.

**

The pub that I arrive outside of at six o'clock has a regal name - The Crown Prince - and I see the man I'm here to meet waiting for me by the entrance, though he's certainly not royalty. He's puffing on a cigarette and hasn't even bothered to change out of his work clothes for the occasion. I can't say I've made much of an effort myself, but, then again, I'm not the one hoping to get lucky tonight, at least not in the bedroom anyway.

'You look lovely,' I'm told in between puffs of nicotine before he stretches out a hand towards me. 'I realised we never properly introduced ourselves earlier. I'm Alan.'

'Gabby,' I say quietly as I reluctantly take his and shake it.

'Right, what would you like to drink, Gabby?' Alan asks as he tosses his cigarette butt to the floor and uses his foot to squash it into the concrete.

'An orange juice will be fine,' I say as Alan opens the door to the pub, but he pauses when he hears my answer.

'That just won't do. You need to have a proper drink. What's your favourite tipple?'

I really would prefer not to drink alcohol, not just because of my past with it but because I'd prefer to keep all my wits about me around this leering man. But he's clearly not going to be as receptive to me and my need for an address unless I play along, so I tell him I'll have some vodka in that orange juice too.

'Good girl,' Alan says before entering the pub and as I follow him in, I see several old men look up to watch us arrive. Alan says hi to a few of them but they're all looking at me more than him, or rather they're all looking at my body.

Some of the men around here really don't care if I'm just a walking bundle of coat, scarf and gloves, do they?

As Alan places our drinks order and the landlord with the tattooed arms gets to work pouring them, I ask about the address again.

'Patience,' Alan tells me before he gratefully accepts his pint of lager and takes a long sip of the frothy liquid.

I receive my vodka and orange and stare down at my drink, not wanting to take a sip if I can help it, and Alan hasn't noticed that I've not yet as he leads me to a table in the corner.

All eyes in the pub are still on us as we take a seat, before Alan tries to get to know me more, enquiring about my love life, which I say little about before turning the question back on him. It turns out he's divorced (a real shocker) and is just looking for a bit of fun these days before he wonders if I might be able to help him with that. I hint that I can, but only if I get the address he promised.

'Okay, you have come out for a drink with me, so here it is,' he says, taking out his phone.

I take mine out too so I can write it down, and as he gives me the address for a property just outside Glasgow, I am already trying to work out how long it will take me to get there.

'It was a nice place, if I remember rightly,' Alan says. 'Big countryside house, middle of nowhere, lots of fields around it. Bet it cost a small fortune. How the other half live, hey?'

Alan winks at me and picks up his drink while I keep staring at the map on my phone and the little red dot where Cara supposedly lives. Now I have what I need, I have to extricate myself from this situation but how do I do it, especially when Alan is clearly settled in for a late night with me?

'How about another drink?' I offer, even though I've barely touched mine and Alan has only had half of his beer. But he doesn't seem to mind and is happy for me to return to the bar, which I do, and once I have our next drinks, I return and hand Alan his second beer.

He quickly downs what was left of his first and starts on his new one, and I'm hoping he keeps on drinking like a fish because that way, he'll need to go to the toilet sooner and that will be when I can sneak out of this pub without him stopping me.

It ends up taking half an hour and Alan buying his third beer, amidst a lot of chatter about him and his ex-wife, before he tells me he needs to pay a visit to the bathroom. He gets up from his seat, groaning as he does, due to all the extra calories he's added to his daily intake, and as he shuffles away to the gent's toilet, I stay in my seat so that everything seems normal.

Alan glances back at me before entering the bathroom and I raise my glass and smile at him when he does. But as soon as he is out of sight then I grab my handbag and phone and get up, ready to make a sharp exit. As I head for the door, I stop and tell one of the other patrons in here, an old man who is watching me walk by, that I am going outside for a cigarette and for him to tell Alan that I'll be back in a moment. The old man nods his head, and I leave the pub, waiting for the door to close before running as fast as I can down the street.

Once I'm a good distance away, I phone for a taxi and as soon as it arrives, I give them my destination.

I'm on my way to Cara's house.

34

I've been in the taxi for thirty minutes, and as I look out through the window, I see nothing but darkness. We left the motorway a while ago and I'm guessing we're now on country lanes, though it's hard to tell. Alan said this house was remote, and he wasn't joking. I can't see any lights outside, only the inky blackness of the Scottish countryside at night to gaze out at as my imagination runs wild.

I check the map on my phone and see that we should reach Cara's house in the next five minutes and as we get closer, I think about how I'm going to play this. I want to observe her house for a short while before knocking on the door and speaking to Cara, just in case there is anything of interest to see that she might otherwise hide if she knows I'm there. That's why I'll ask my driver to drop me off a little further back from the house, so that I can approach on foot under the cover of dark.

I'll tell my taxi driver to leave rather than wait because I have no idea how long I'll be, and that means there is a risk that I'll end up stranded out here if I can't get another taxi to come and pick me up again. I may not have a phone signal, and depending on what happens with Cara and whether or not I'm right or wrong about her, she may not be willing to call me a cab with her landline phone, but I'll just have to deal with that problem if and when it happens.

The quiet driver who I've been travelling with from Stirling eventually indicates to turn off this remote country lane, and as I see us entering a long, narrow driveway, I realise this is the start of where Cara's property begins.

'You can just drop me off here, thank you,' I say, and the driver gently taps the brakes, bringing us to a stop.

'Are you sure? It looks like the house is still a bit of a walk away from here,' he tells me, but I tell him it's fine, before paying the fare and getting out.

As the taxi leaves, I watch the lights from the vehicle growing dimmer and dimmer until they disappear completely. A bird crows in the distance, and I feel a little nervous being out here by myself, so I start walking quickly, following the path that leads towards the looming property I can just about make out in the distance.

As I get closer, I see lights on inside the house, as well as a car parked on the driveway, and I find myself a tree to stand behind to give myself some cover should anybody look out. Watching the windows, I look out for signs of movement inside.

I expect Cara to be in here, but is anybody else with her?

A partner? A child?

My child?

Alan was right, this place is huge and must have cost a fortune, though I'm sure the proceeds from the sale of the house in Buckingham Place paid off a lot of this. It must be cheaper to live out here in the middle of nowhere rather than in a city, and I wonder what it is that Cara does for work. But that's not all I'm wondering, and as I keep watching the various windows, I am thinking about what is going on inside.

My as-yet-unproven theory that Cara sold her house because she had something to do with Tuppence going missing across the road from her front door gains strength when I think about how this would be the perfect place to hide if she had committed a crime. There are no other houses around for miles, no neighbours to see what she is doing, nobody to notice that she might be harbouring the little girl who captured the nation's attention when everybody wanted to know where she was.

There's a sudden flash of dark hair through one of the windows and while it was brief, I see it again a moment later. The second time is when I realise that I'm looking at Cara. She looks a little different to how she appears in her Facebook photo. Her hair is slightly shorter and she's wearing a baggy sweatshirt as opposed to the tighter clothing she is pictured in online, but I presume she might have been younger then and looking to impress the opposite sex more. Does she have a boyfriend or husband now? I keep watching, but there is no sign of anybody, at least until I hear the faint sound of a car engine approaching in the distance.

Crouching down and making sure I'm fully out of view from whoever is coming, I watch the two headlights getting nearer to the house until the car passes right by where I am hiding behind the tree.

As the car parks, I stand back up, confident I'm not at risk of being seen, and I watch to see who gets out of the vehicle. But before anybody can get out, the front door opens and Cara emerges, rushing towards the car with a big smile on her face. But she doesn't approach the driver's side, instead going to one of the back doors and after opening it, she reaches in and I can't quite see what she is doing for a moment.

When I do see her again, I gasp.

She has a young girl in her arms.

It's dark, I'm at a distance and time has passed since I last saw her but right there, in that moment, something in my body screams at me that this toddler is my daughter.

I almost cry out for Tuppence, the sixth sense inside me fully believing this is my baby. I want to run over there, snatch her from that woman's arms and run back out into the darkness, escaping this isolated place and the evil people who took my daughter from me. But for now, I stay sensible and keep watch and I see Cara carrying the child into the house. Just behind her, the driver's side door opens, and a man gets out from behind the wheel to follow the rest of his family members inside.

But when I see who it is, I physically retch because it can't possibly be so.

The man walking into the house with that woman and child is known to me.

It's Leon.

35

'No,' I say as my stomach churns, and I grip the tree as if not doing so will result in me falling over and being unable to get back to my feet again.

'How can this be possible?' I say, my voice strained, my heart thumping and eyes stinging with tears. I go to gag again, and while nothing happens, I still feel more nauseous than I've ever felt before in my life.

My ex is here with this woman who lived opposite where Tuppence was taken.

That has to be my daughter with them then, which means this has to have all been planned.

'Urghh,' I let out a groan as I grip my stomach and try to stop myself from passing out. But there's too much adrenaline coursing around my body, so maybe I'm more likely to suffer a panic attack than fall unconscious.

How could this be possible? My partner was involved in the abduction of our child?

How did he do it? How did they do it?

How does he even know this woman?

My mind goes back to that street, how Leon and I had walked along it on our first night in Stirling, pushing the pram and admiring all the homes we walked by. Had he been there before? Is that why he led me down there? To be closer to Cara? Was he having an affair with her before we even went to Stirling? Was the whole trip really just an opportunity for them to take my baby and play happy families themselves?

I stare at the house but see no more signs of movement, though I know all three are in there now. Most of all, *she* is in there. Tuppence, my daughter. She looked so big, so different to the last time I held her, but it was her, of course it was. Leon is here, her daddy, still looking out for her, getting the opportunity of caring for her that I have been denied of for so long.

He told me he had taken a new job in The Highlands. Another lie, clearly done to throw me off the scent. If I thought my ex-husband was in a totally different part of Scotland, I would never suspect he was actually here, near Glasgow, living in a remote house with our child and a woman who lived opposite where she was taken.

I have to know how they did this, what the plan was, how they pulled it off, how they have gotten away with it for so long.

I want to call the police and see Leon and Cara in handcuffs as soon as possible, but the lack of signal on my phone means I can't do that. The nearest available phone I could use will be inside that house, but I can hardly just walk in and ask to use it, can I?

What would I say?

"Hi, Leon, remember me? Is that our daughter? She looks well considering she was abducted. Do you mind if I use your phone so I can have you and your evil lover arrested?"

That's not quite how this is supposed to work, but as I stare at the house, I begin to think that even if I could call the police, that would be too good for this couple. Being arrested is the easy way out for them. I want revenge, which is why I start walking towards the house, my pace quickening the nearer I get to it.

As I reach Leon's car, I want to smash the windows on it, let down the tyres, destroy it, but that would only alert those inside of my presence, and I want to catch them off guard. Walking past his car and then Cara's, I approach one of the windows and carefully peer in. When I do, I see what looks like a playroom full of toys, all of them scattered around on a rug. But there's no one in there, so I move onto the next window, and that's where I find this fake family.

The three of them are snuggled up together on the sofa, Cara and Leon on either side of Tuppence - him eating from a large bag of crisps, her turning up the volume on the television. They're watching some cartoon, presumably one of Tuppence's favourites, and I find myself staring at the little girl's face as her eyes excitedly take in the moving images on the screen.

I keep watching for what must be at least half an hour until Cara turns the television off and picks up Tuppence before taking her out of the room. I want to know where they have gone, but I watch Leon for a moment too, how he just lies there on the sofa, eating a few more crisps whilst checking his phone. How the hell can he be so casual about what he's done, as if he doesn't have a care in the world? Then again, he thinks I'm back in Edinburgh and will never find this place.

If only he knew I was right outside.

I walk around the rest of the house then, looking in other windows but failing to see Cara and Tuppence. I guess she's taken my daughter upstairs, possibly to bath her before bed, and it is certainly around the time a child her age should be getting put down for the night.

I wonder what Tuppence is like now. Does she sleep through until sunrise, or does she wake during the hours of darkness for extra feeds and hugs? If it's the latter, Cara is the one on hand to give them. I bet Leon stays asleep, just like he did with me. I doubt he's suddenly become a new man, although Cara certainly looked happy enough with him on the sofa a few moments ago.

I notice Leon heading for the stairs and watch as he goes up, and that confirms that it must be Tuppence's bedtime and he is going to lend a hand. With everyone upstairs, I quickly look for a way in downstairs, but all the doors are locked. Not wanting to be out here all night while everyone in the house sleeps, I need to find a way to draw somebody out so I might be able to sneak in momentarily, and that's when I return to Leon's car.

Trying the handle on the driver's side door, it's obviously locked, but I keep pulling and messing with it until I activate the loud car alarm that is meant to deter thieves. With the alarm deafening in an area as quiet as this one, I race to the side of the house and hide, waiting for Leon to come out and check on his car. It doesn't take him long to do that and as he leaves the house and walks down to his car, nervously looking around to see what might have set the alarm off, I wait for my chance.

Leon reaches his car and takes a closer look at it but finds no damage because I was careful not to leave any. But, with his back turned to the house, he isn't able to see me run inside and while I hear the car alarm turn off, it's already too late for the car owner.

I'm inside the house now.

Eager to find a hiding place quickly, I see a cupboard under the stairs and rush towards it, opening the door and getting in before shutting it behind me and doing my best to hide behind the coats that hang in here. There is a musty smell around me, one of sweaty shoes, but I don't care about that as I remain in my hiding place.

I hear the front door shut before Leon calls upstairs to let Cara know that everything is okay. Then he asks if she needs some help, but she calls down that she is fine, and I hear my ex-husband's footsteps move past the cupboard. Then I hear the clinking of a bottle, and I guess Leon has just decided to treat himself to a beer after a busy day.

The footsteps move past the cupboard again before I hear the low volume of the TV in the background, a football match being put on. *Leon really has it easy here.*

More footsteps can be heard a few minutes later, loud ones right above my head, and I assume it's Cara coming back down the stairs. She must have got Tuppence to sleep and is now coming down to enjoy her evening with her man.

I hear the two of them talking, though I can't quite make out what is being said. More noises follow. The sound of a microwave in use. A kettle boiling. Pots and pans being moved around and a little later, knives and forks scraping on plates. They must be having their evening meal, and Leon washes it down with another beer from the fridge, judging by the sound of a bottle top being popped open.

My legs are sore from standing for so long, and my neck and back are aching from the uncomfortable hiding place I have squeezed myself into, but finally, after a few hours, I hear the TV go off and then footsteps moving above me.

Leon and Cara have gone up to bed now.

Soon they'll be asleep.

That's when it'll be time for me to leave my hiding place.

36

It's not so much the sound I'm making with my feet as I creep up the stairs that worries me, as it is my breathing, because the latter is far louder in this silent house.

I just can't help it, it's impossible to breathe quietly when I'm in such a stressful, emotional situation. I'm stressed because I'm sneaking around a house that doesn't belong to me in the dead of night, and I'm emotional because I know every step I take is bringing me a little closer to my daughter.

As I reach the top of the stairs, I can hear the faint sound of a white noise machine and I follow it to a bedroom door, behind which is the room I presume Tuppence is in. The door is slightly ajar, so I carefully give it a push and it opens easily, the white noise becoming louder as it does.

The background noise gives me a little leeway in how quiet I have to be and should hopefully cover up the sound of any slight creaking from the floorboards beneath me, or my breathing, if it continues to get heavier. It certainly does when I lay eyes on the crib in the far corner of the room, the bed sitting there in the soft glow of an orange bedside lamp.

I know Tuppence is in there, so I go to step forward and see her, but I freeze when I notice the camera next to her crib, positioned so that it is facing where the child sleeps and can capture anything that happens in and around the crib itself. Cara and Leon have obviously decided to play it safe and have their child's sleep monitored so they can be alerted if there are any issues in the night, and that is sensible. It is exactly what I would have been doing. It's also going to cause me a big problem because how can I pick Tuppence up and get her out of here without them seeing me and coming in here to stop me?

Looking around the room, I see it is a perfectly safe environment for a child to have as their bedroom. No sharp edges, no choking hazards, nothing that could fall into the crib and suffocate the sleeping child. Just some fluffy toys on a shelf across the room, a changing mat on the floor and some animal stencils of lions and zebras stuck to the walls. So this is where my daughter has been, at least for a big part of the time she has been missing. It's still criminal what Leon and Cara have done, but it is somewhat of a relief that my child has been here, in this pleasant environment, rather than in any one of the god-awful places I had imagined her being in, the worst of which was a ditch by the side of a road.

I want nothing more than to pick up my girl and feel her again, but I'm not sure if all the extra movement in the crib will set off an alarm in the adults' bedroom and see them come in here to check it out. Some parents have monitors to detect when there might be a problem in the night.

I am certainly a problem.

What would I do if they caught me here? I dread to think because I'm still so angry and shocked, so it wouldn't be good, whatever happened.

It wouldn't be good for the people who caught me.

But I can't just stand here all night and do nothing either.

Something has to give, and after all this time, I have no other choice.

Screw it, I'm getting my baby back.

I move towards the crib, caring less about the camera with each step I take, and when I look inside, I see my darling daughter fast asleep. She looks so peaceful, so unaware of the horror that has already taken place in her life. Maybe she did know for a while, crying when she missed me, but perhaps she soon got over that when she realised that her father was around, finding comfort in his familiar face, totally oblivious to the fact that by taking her, he was stealing her from me.

Unlike the last time I stood over a baby's crib, I don't need to send off for a DNA test because I just know this is my child. Not only does she look like me but I just feel it in my bones, a deep-rooted motherly instinct that this is the little life that grew inside me for nine months. When Tuppence was first born, I used to ask Leon if he thought we would recognise our daughter in a room full of other newborns just like her. I mean, a lot of the time, babies look pretty similar at first glance, so it felt like a valid question. But I very quickly realised how stupid it was because of course I would recognise my own daughter, no matter how similar she looked to however many other children she might have been surrounded by. That's because it's not just about the outer appearance but the intangibles too; the eye contact, the subtle facial expressions, the scent, the feeling that emanates from your heart when you are in the presence of someone you love so much. That's how I know this is Tuppence, and that is why I am now picking her up and preparing to get the hell out of this house with her as quickly as I can.

Ignoring the camera, I hold her carefully in my arms and, bless her, she doesn't even wake. She's heavy, but I wouldn't drop her for anything, not now, not ever, and I don't even flinch when I accidentally knock the side of the crib with my thigh and send a sharp jolt of pain through that part of my body. But the movement and the noise does cause Tuppence to stir a little and her eyes open slightly, looking up at mine and making me nervous.

Will she recognise me?

Or will she scream?

I'd be heartbroken if she was to do the latter, though I couldn't blame her because she hasn't seen me for so long and she surely only expects to see Cara or Leon's face when she first wakes up. But she's barely awake at all, and her eyes close again quickly, telling me she at least feels settled in my arms, and that's enough for me for the time being.

I turn away from the crib and head for the bedroom door but as I do, I hear something in another room. It's a musical chime, a pleasant sound, childlike but enough to wake a sleeping parent up, and the point of it is to wake them up. I know it's sounding because the camera will have detected too much movement in the crib, and when either Cara or Leon wake, they will check the camera beside their bed and see exactly what has happened.

The crib is now empty.

I have even less time to waste than I did before, so I reach the door and rush out into the hallway. As I go, my quicker movements wake Tuppence up and she starts to cry, her peaceful slumber disturbed. The crying is sure to wake the adults in the other bedroom, and just as I reach the stairs, I hear footsteps approaching.

Spinning around, I see a bedroom door shoot open and suddenly, I'm face to face with the woman who took my baby.

'Leon!' Cara cries when she sees me standing out in the darkness with a restless Tuppence in my arms.

I hear scrambling in the room behind her and a second later, my ex-husband appears. When he sees me, his mouth visibly hangs open in shock.

'You took her from me!' I scream at him, aware that my loud voice won't do anything to settle Tuppence's cries, but I have to vent some of my fury at these people.

'What the hell are you doing here?' Leon asks, as if there's no good reason for me to make an appearance, which is ludicrous.

'I'm taking back my daughter!' I cry defiantly. 'Then I'm calling the police and having both of you arrested!'

I turn back to the stairs then and start descending, careful not to go too fast and lose my footing on the steps, because I can't risk falling with Tuppence, but still trying to go quick enough so I'm not caught. But it's not fast enough, and I feel a hand on my arm trying to pull me back.

Instinctively, I swing, and the back of my hand connects with the face of the person who was trying to stop me. I expect it was Leon but as I look, I see it was actually Cara who came after me, although I only get a brief glimpse of her. That's because the force of the blow I just dealt her has seen her topple to the side and go straight through the bannister at this part of the top of the stairs.

She cries out as she falls, and she only goes quiet when her head hits the hard hallway floor below.

As I look down, I see she is not moving.

Leon sees it too.

Tuppence is still crying.

And now, for the first time in a long time, *it's just the three of us again.*

37

As I keep hold of Tuppence and try to quieten her cries, more for her sake than anyone else's, Leon rushes past me down the stairs. He reaches Cara, who still hasn't moved, and tries to shake her awake. When that doesn't work, he calls her name, and after that has delivered no response either, he checks her neck for a pulse. Only then does he stop trying and look up at me standing on the staircase above him.

'She's dead,' he says quietly, his voice only just audible above the crying coming from the little girl in my arms.

I'm not sure what the appropriate response should be to that news. Shock? Horror? Denial? Panic? Most people would probably freak out if they had just killed somebody, even if it was accidental. But I genuinely don't care about that woman's body and if anything, her out of the way is just one less obstacle between me and getting Tuppence out of here.

But Leon is far more emotional about it and tries to stir Cara several more times, despite him already knowing it's futile. I guess she banged her head in the fall. My slap caused that fall, but how was I to know she would go over the staircase and land heavily below? It's her fault this happened. She came after me to try and stop me, and I wouldn't have even been here if she hadn't done what she had.

'Tell me how you did it,' I say calmly as Leon gives up and sits with his back against the hallway wall, his head in his hands, his head that he keeps shaking as if he can't process what has happened. But when he fails to answer me, I walk down the stairs and go for the door, willing to walk away from this chaotic scene and get Tuppence somewhere safer.

'Wait! Where are you going?' Leon calls out, lifting his head up and aghast that I'm leaving him here.

'Where do you think I'm going? I'm taking my daughter home, and I'm getting the police to come and arrest you!'

'But you killed her! You can't call the police. You'll go to prison too.'

I really should just walk out the door, but the fact that Leon thinks he can try and get himself out of trouble by making me worry about my own consequences is infuriating.

'You two stole a baby!' I say as Tuppence stops crying, possibly because the loud voices have startled her into silence. 'She is mine, right? This is our daughter. You took her from me. You and that bitch!'

I wait to hear what kind of crazy explanation Leon might have for doing what he did, or even hear him try and deny it and say that it isn't Tuppence who I am currently holding. But he doesn't do any of that. He just starts crying.

'I'm so sorry,' he says. 'I messed up. I don't know what I was thinking.'

Then he goes and says something I wasn't expecting.

'It was her idea,' he says before burying his head in his hands again.

Her idea?

I look at Cara, the way she fell, the way her neck is twisted slightly, the way her arms are splayed out at her sides, and I realise I'm never going to get her side of the story, no matter what happens from here. She won't be interviewed by the police or put on trial or forced to give me her explanation. I only have Leon to give me that and maybe, if I walk away now, I will never know what truly happened, especially not if Leon does something stupid to avoid going to prison, something like hurting himself before the police can get here.

I need to know what happened and this might end up being my only chance, so with that in mind, I walk away from the front door and tell Leon that we have to talk in the kitchen right now.

Taking a seat at the table, I balance Tuppence on my knee, but she quickly grows restless, so I tell Leon to get her some of her toys from the playroom. He does that, moving slowly and wearily, but once he hands Tuppence a rattle, she is happy enough to shake it and entertain herself for a little while at least. She's still calm with me, not wanting her daddy or anybody else, which only makes me feel proud of her love for me yet angry that I've been denied it for so long.

'Sit down and start talking,' I say to my ex-husband, and he does as I tell him, easing himself into the chair opposite me before putting his elbows on the table and supporting his head in his hands once again. It's as if he no longer possesses the strength to lift his own head up, but maybe he doesn't. Then again, it must be hard, if not impossible, to look me in the eye after what he has done to our family.

'It started on the second night we were in Stirling,' Leon says quietly, so I tell him to speak up over the sound of Tuppence's rattle. 'It was the first night I took Tuppence for a walk by myself. Do you remember? You were the one who suggested I take her on my own while you went to go back to wash some milk bottles.'

'I remember.'

'I took her the way we went that first night together. Around the streets. Onto Buckingham Place.'

'And…'

'That was where I met Cara.'

I frown because I'm not quite following. 'She lived in the house opposite where Tuppence was taken,' I say, and Leon nods. 'How did you meet her?' I ask then.

'She was on her driveway as I passed with the pram. She was trying to get a bag out of her car, but she was struggling and when I saw her, I offered to help.'

'You offered to help? I wonder why.'

Leon has always had a soft spot for pretty brunettes, and I know because he fell for me at one point.

'I was just trying to help,' he insists, looking up at me for a split second before looking away again. 'I pushed the pram to her front door then carried the bag inside for her.'

'Then what happened?'

'She was smiling at Tuppence. Said how cute she was and how it was nice to see the dad out with the pram because she only ever saw mums pushing their babies around here. Then she asked me where Tuppence's mother was.'

'And what did you say?'

'I said you were at home. I don't know, it must have been the way I said it or something, but Cara seemed to detect that we were having problems.'

Problems would be an understatement, but that's not the point.

'You hinted that you were unhappy? To do what? Get this new woman to think she had a chance with you?'

'No, it wasn't like that,' Leon tries, but I am too wise to believe any of his nonsense, so I just shake my head and tell him to get on with it.

'I don't really know how it happened. One minute we were just talking, the next I was inside with her.'

'You cheated on me while our daughter was in your care?'

'No, I mean, well, not exactly.'

'What the hell happened?'

'Cara invited me in. I left Tuppence asleep in her pram in Cara's hallway. Then we went upstairs.'

'You've got to be kidding me.'

I stare at the pathetic excuse of a man that I married and wonder how I could ever have been so dumb as to fall in love with him before.

'It was crazy. I don't know what to say. It was just lust. Stupid nonsense. It was over so quick. Neither one of us had done anything like that before.'

I think back to that second night in Stirling and then it dawns on me.

'That was the night you were late coming back,' I realise. 'You were out for over an hour, and I was angry when you got home. I'd been thinking you'd had an accident but all that time, you were with another woman!'

I'd throw something at Leon if it wasn't for the fact that Tuppence is in my arms, but she starts crying again, frightened by my loud shouting, and despite trying to calm her again, she only settles when Leon offers to take her. But I refuse to give her up, so the best compromise I can make is to put her down on the floor with some more of her toys.

'So what happened next?' I want to know. 'How did you go from having sex to abducting a baby?'

Leon seems reluctant to speak again, but he has no choice unless he wants me to leave here and go straight to the police, and after I remind him of that, he's soon talking again.

'The next day, the day we'd been up to the castle. It had been a good day.'

I recall that third day in Stirling, and Leon is right, it had been a good day. In fact, it had been a great day, the best day of the entire holiday and the first time I'd thought there was a real chance the two of us might be able to make things work after all. But then it dawns on me just why Leon had been in such a good mood.

'You were still on a high after sleeping with her, weren't you?' I realise, shaking my head in disgust. 'There I was thinking you were making more of an effort to be a better husband and father, but secretly, you were just happy because you'd been with another woman the night before and gotten away with it.'

Leon can try and tell me it's not like that all he wants, but I just tell him to move on by pre-empting what happened next.

'You volunteered to take Tuppence on her pre-bedtime walk that third night,' I remember. 'Please tell me you didn't go back to Cara's house.'

Leon doesn't answer that, which is an answer in itself, and now, with my hands free without Tuppence in them, I reach for the nearest thing I can find to throw at him, which just so happens to be Tuppence's rattle.

The toy hits Leon's shoulder, and he grimaces before getting up, clearly worried that I'm going to throw something worse at him next. But the kitchen knives are just out of my reach, so he's safe, for the moment anyway.

'Did you sleep with her again that next night?' I demand to know, and Leon solemnly nods his head, which prompts another outburst from me. 'You're unbelievable! You're disgusting!'

I want to go for the knives now, and the only thing stopping me is the fact I can't kill Leon in the presence of our child. That thought makes me stop and think for a second, and I remember more about that third night we had in Stirling.

'You went out that night,' I recall. 'You said there was a guitarist playing in a pub nearby and you asked for permission to go out for a few beers. Did you really go to a pub, or did you go back to her house again while I stayed at home and looked after our baby?'

'No, I didn't go to her house, I went to the pub,' Leon tells me, and that's something I suppose, at least it is until he finishes his statement. 'But Cara was in the pub too. We had arranged to meet.'

Leon's lies know no bounds, but before I can say anything more, he speaks again.

'That was where we came up with the plan.'

'The plan?' I repeat, staring at the shell of the man I once married.

'Yes,' Leon says quietly. 'The plan to take Tuppence and start a new life away from you.'

38

Could this be any more of a bizarre situation? I'm sitting in someone else's house, having just found my kidnapped child, listening to my husband tell me all about a criminal plot while the body of his co-conspirator lies on the floor in the next room. But if I thought things were crazy, I hadn't even heard what Leon and Cara did yet.

'I never should have gone to the pub that night,' Leon says, as if everything he had done before that moment was totally fine. 'That was the night when I started to really lose control of myself and what I was doing.'

'Whose idea was it to take Tuppence?' I ask, not caring for Leon's sob story, only the facts.

'Cara's,' he confirms. 'She told me that she couldn't have children herself, but she had always wanted a little girl. I felt sorry for her, I could see she was upset about it. But then she suggested, based on how unhappy my own marriage was and the fact that I'd already embarked on this affair, that we take Tuppence and make a family of our own.'

'And you thought that was a good idea?'

'No, of course not. I mean, not right away. I couldn't see how it was possible. I told Cara that if I was to divorce you, you would surely get custody of Tuppence, so whatever idealistic plan Cara had probably wouldn't work out. But then she told me that she wasn't thinking of me asking you for a divorce and trying to get custody. She was thinking of just taking Tuppence and getting away with it.'

Leon's expression can best be described as haunted as he carries on.

'I thought Cara was joking at first,' he says. 'I mean, it sounded ridiculous. Taking a baby and getting away with it. Who does that? But then she told me how we would do it.'

I already know how they did it at this point, or at least the nuts and bolts of it, but I stay quiet and allow Leon to describe every grim detail.

'She told me to get you to take Tuppence out in the pram that next night, and I was to call her when you were on your way to Buckingham Place. That's why I stayed home, pretending to be too hungover to go with you. Then Cara got in position, hiding in the back garden of the house opposite hers and waiting for me to text her when you were outside.'

'You were following me that night?'

Leon nods his head but is too ashamed to look at me as he does. He can't even look at Tuppence either, so he makes do with staring at the wall behind me.

'When I saw you were outside that house, I texted Cara and then she started the fake cries for help. That street was always so quiet, Cara knew you would hear the calls and go and investigate, and you did. Cara had put the bins in the way so you couldn't take the pram with you, and when you left Tuppence for a moment, I quickly took her and ran across the street and into Cara's home.'

Leon's speaking perfect English, but what he is saying is just so unfathomable that I'm having a hard time understanding it.

'You took our baby and ran away with her?' I repeat back. 'You allowed me to find the pram empty and go through hell, all for what? So you could have a fling with some woman you'd just met.'

'I know, it's stupid and illegal and immoral and whatever else you want to call it,' Leon says sadly. 'But she wasn't just some woman. She made me happy. She made me feel like we used to feel.'

'You and her should be locked up and you both would be if she was still alive!' I cry. 'But at least you can pay for this!'

'No, please, Gabby! Just calm down. We can work this out.'

Leon's suggestion of working this out is laughable, but the only thing stopping me from leaving now is because I still don't quite know what happened after he took Tuppence.

'I don't understand. Where did you hide her?' I ask. 'How could she have been in Cara's home? The police searched everywhere on that street, including inside all the houses.'

'There was a hidden room in that house that no one knew about,' Leon says. 'Cara told me that it didn't show up on any plans because it was constructed so long ago and only the family who lived there knew of it. The house had been in her family for generations. She'd inherited it from her parents who passed away several years ago. The property was full of little eccentricities and one of them was a small sound-proof room behind a bookcase. It was crazy, like something you might see in a movie. But it was the perfect place to hide a baby. That's where I put Tuppence.'

The thought that the police were so close to finding my daughter yet so far is galling, and I think about how I spent hours stood out on that street praying for a development when little did I know my baby girl was only a few yards away, in a house nearby, behind a bookcase, crying out for me in a sound-proof room.

'With Tuppence hidden, I left Cara's place via the back garden,' Leon goes on. 'That got me out onto the next street, and I just waited there until you phoned me to tell me she had gone missing.'

'That was why you got there so quickly,' I recall. 'I thought you'd sprinted to get to me, but you were close by all that time.'

This just gets worse and worse, I think, but there's still something I'm unsure of.

'How did Cara get back to her house without me seeing her?' I ask. 'If she was in that back garden across the road and I was standing out in the middle of the street, how did she slip past me?'

'She worked her way to her house carefully, while you were talking to other neighbours. It was dark and she stuck to the back gardens. No one saw her and we figured you wouldn't be in a great state of mind, so you wouldn't be fully aware of what was going on around you. She made it back before the police came and with Tuppence hidden away, Cara let them search her house knowing nothing would be found.'

'And you just stood with me all that time and pretended to be as shocked and heartbroken as I was,' I say, shaking my head in disgust. 'You even faked being mad at me. I thought you hated me for losing her, but all that time, you were just putting on an act.'

'I don't know what to say,' Leon admits. 'Except that I'm terribly sorry and I hope you can forgive me.'

Leon must think I'm the most stupid woman in the world if I was to ever forgive him, but rather than make it obvious that there's no chance of that happening, I have to consider what I do next.

'So what happened then?' I ask.

'Cara kept Tuppence hidden away until things died down a little on the street and with the police investigation. Then I took her one night. I rented a place where no one knew me, and no one had any idea that Tuppence was the missing baby in the news. That was when I told you I was moving away to The Highlands. Cara put her house on the market after that, a good time after so as not to arouse too much suspicion, and when it eventually sold, she bought this place. The idea was we would live here as a family for as long as we could.'

'What the hell would you have done when Tuppence grew up? How could you have kept her identity a secret then?'

'We would have changed her name. She wouldn't remember any of what happened, of course, so I guess there was a chance we could have done it. I don't know. It seems so stupid now, but Cara was persuasive.

She wanted to do anything to make it work. She wanted to do anything to have what we had.'

'What we had?'

'A family unit. The joy of parenting. She didn't have that for herself. She had a huge house and a lot of generational wealth passed down to her, but she didn't have a child or a partner. Not until she met me. I suppose I wanted what she was offering too. A quiet life with a woman who just wanted to have fun with me rather than hate me. Cara didn't know about my past, my mistakes. She bore no grudges. There was no history for us to awkwardly try and work through. It was just more enjoyable, I suppose. More optimistic. Simpler.'

'Simpler?' I cry, disgusted at my ex-husband's choice of word. 'For you, maybe, but not for me. I've been through hell trying to find out what happened to my daughter!'

Then I think about the dead woman in the hallway and how her desperation to get what she wanted by any means necessary has led to her downfall, as well as Leon's. But while she has paid the price for what she did, the man sitting across from me at this table has not and he knows it.

'What are you going to do?' Leon asks me nervously. 'With the police, I mean.'

'What do you want me to do?' I ask calmly, aware I hold all the power here.

'Don't call them. Don't tell them what I did. We can cover this up. Find a way to keep our family together. If not for my sake or yours, then for Tuppence's. She deserves to have both her parents around to raise her. If I go to prison for this, that means she will grow up without a father, and who knows how much that will mess her up when she's an adult.'

The gall on Leon to try and guilt me into not reporting him to the police simply for our daughter's sake beggar's belief, but I'm also aware that in his distressed, anxious state, he won't allow me to just calmly pick up the phone and call to have him arrested. He'd keep trying to stop me, and how far would he go to do that? I could be in danger, so maybe it's better if I come around to his way of thinking.

'What do we do about Cara?' I ask. 'Her body.'

'I could hide it,' Leon says, perking up when he senses that I'm giving him a chance here. 'There's lots of land around here. I could bury her, and no one would ever find her.'

'Then what? We just carry on living here? As if that will work.'

'We could do it! We're so remote, nobody ever comes to the house. I could just carry on doing what I've been doing, going into town, buying groceries, bringing them back here. Cara has no family. Her parents are dead; she has no siblings, so no one will look for her. You know what it's like in certain parts of Scotland, people live a quiet life, totally off the grid. We could do the same. I'll keep working while you look after our daughter. We could last for years out here.'

I listen to everything Leon has to say before making my decision.

'I'll stay with Tuppence,' I say calmly. 'While you get rid of the body.'

Leon thanks me for my compassion before springing into action, clearly eager to have the body disposed of before the sun comes up in a few hours. While he rushes around, putting on his boots and a pair of gloves and pulling out a spade from the garage, I take Tuppence back upstairs to try and get her settled. While there, I hear Leon dragging Cara's body out of the house before I hear a car engine start. Looking out of the window with my sleeping baby in my arms, I see Leon driving out into the field at the back of the house before he eventually comes to a stop near a row of trees that I can only just make out in the murkiness of night.

That must be the spot he has decided on for Cara's final resting place, and I wonder how long it will take him to dig her grave. Not wanting to wait too long, I carefully place Tuppence down in her crib and with her settled, I rush downstairs and look for a letter with this house address on. I find one then go to the house phone, where I make an emergency call, and when the operator answers, I quickly tell them what the problem is.

'Help! You need to send the police immediately. My ex-husband has killed somebody and he's currently burying her body! He's the father of Tuppence Hartley, the child who went missing in Stirling. He took her, him and his mistress. I'm the mother and Tuppence is safe, but only if you get here before he comes back to the house.'

Then I give the operator the address on the letter and am told to stay on the line until help arrives. I do just that, praying that they will get here before Leon has finished hiding the body.

It would be great if they could catch him in the act.

It would be great if I could get my revenge on him after what he has done to this family.

39

There aren't many greater joys in life than watching your child interacting with your mother, and that is a joy I am currently experiencing as I watch Mum and Tuppence playing with toys together.

I smile at the pair and feel grateful to be able to witness such a thing as two generations of my family coming together, and I also feel relief, not just for me but for Mum. When Tuppence was gone, she had ceased to be a grandmother, but now she is back doing what she does best, caring for a little one, showering them with love and affection and helping mould them into a fine person who will hopefully have a positive impact on the world one day.

It's good to have Tuppence home, or at least the place I currently call home, which is not the place my child was first growing up in but the place I moved into when everything was turned on its head. The flat we're in is quickly becoming cramped now that it's filled with Tuppence's belongings and is nowhere near as spacious as the home we used to share with Leon before we made that trip to Stirling and all the drama began. But it will do for now, until I can figure out something better. All that matters is that my daughter is here because home for me will always be wherever she is.

As for my ex-husband, his current home is a prison wing about fifty miles from here, which is where he is currently being held while he awaits sentencing for all the heinous acts he has committed. I didn't have any qualms about calling the police that night, and it was a relief when they arrived and I pointed them out to the field where Leon was busy digging a hole to hide a dead body. He never got to finish that hole because he was put in handcuffs and taken away, his face as pale as a Scottish sky at sunrise as he was led past me, whatever dreams he once had about the three of us somehow making it all work again dashed in the blink of an eye.

I haven't seen him since, nor do I care to see him ever again, though our paths may cross one more time if I have to go to court and talk about what he and Cara did to us. I'll do that if necessary, whatever helps get him the longest prison sentence possible, but it remains to be seen because so far, Leon has admitted to his part in the abduction, so he's going away for a long time regardless, even before the dead body he was discovered with is taken into account. But interestingly, and perhaps as one final act of repentance on his part, Leon has not told the police that I struck the fatal blow to Cara that saw her fall from the stairs. I just told the police that there had been a scuffle on the stairs and I wasn't really sure what happened, which would potentially cover me if Leon had told them it was me who hit Cara. But he didn't do that, telling them that after I had arrived at the house and tried to take Tuppence back, Cara had got violent and Leon had stepped in to defend me.

I suppose he owed me that at least.

As Mum and Tuppence continue to play, I leave the room to make myself a cup of tea, the mad events of the last few weeks swirling around in my head as I go. No sooner had the police arrested Leon and I had been taken to the station with Tuppence, the media got hold of the events at that farmhouse, and given the scale of the story, it was no surprise that it was quickly making headline news around Scotland.

Missing child found!

Mum gets her baby back!

Daughter's dramatic disappearance - The father did it!

The sensationalist headlines helped sell plenty of newspapers, but while the journalists were able to run all sorts of stories and get away with potentially bending a few truths here and there, the police only cared for hard facts and evidence. That was why one of the first things done was a DNA test, which was taken to prove without doubt that the child I had been found with was really mine.

I knew it in my heart, but it took a piece of paper to confirm it, the test results proving with 99.9% accuracy that the girl was Tuppence. That was when Detective Jacobs got involved, liaising with the police at the station in Glasgow where I was being held while the whole sorry story was being unravelled.

Jacobs, along with Detective McAndrews, questioned me about how it was I was able to track down Tuppence to that farmhouse. I guess I couldn't blame them for wanting to make sure that I really was as innocent in the whole thing as I claimed I was, and there's no doubt it would have seemed a little far-fetched for me to have uncovered Leon and Cara's crimes in the way I was saying I did. But I just simply told the truth – how I read Cameron's book and after discovering the plotline he had about the house sale, I checked for sales on Buckingham Place and saw that one house had been sold in the past year. I told them how I used my very basic and naïve investigating skills to get Cara's name and then how I found out where she was living, and then, I simply went to the house to see if my child was there. I could have easily been disappointed when I got to that house and seen nothing that suggested Tuppence was around, but that's not what happened, and I explained how I saw Leon and knew something awful had occurred behind my back.

The detectives were almost as shocked at my story as all the people who were reading the morning newspapers beside their bowls of cereal, but I was telling the truth, and they must have seen that because they eventually believed me and told me there would be no charges brought against me. I was then free to go home with Tuppence, which I did with great happiness, and ever since then, I've been trying to give my daughter some semblance of a normal life again.

What's it like being reunited with a lost child? It's such a unique and unusual situation that I'm not sure there are any guidelines or rules to follow for the parent. It's more about trying to do what I was doing before I lost Tuppence and that is simply making sure she is getting what she needs on a daily basis. Sustenance, warmth, activity, love. As long as she is smiling, I know I'm doing a good job, and that's all I can do.

There will come a day, many years from now but it is coming, when Tuppence will be old enough to read the news stories that were written about her and her parents. That's why, before that day comes, I will have to sit her down and tell her everything, from beginning to end, without missing out a single thing, so that she is fully prepared for when she has to face that story as she ages. Children at her school might tease her, and some low-life journalists might try and interview her, and there's no doubt she's going to need to be resilient to deal with all of that. That's all before she reaches full maturity and may need some form of counselling to help her process her unorthodox earlier life.

It's bizarre but for a brief period, my daughter, at a tender age, was one of the most famous people in Scotland. Her story will always follow her around, her name forever associated with a dark chapter in Stirling's history, and I bet the real-life documentary based on her and her parents is already being pitched to television studios who are blinded by visions of big ratings and big money. But that's all ahead of us, and we'll deal with each and every obstacle as they pop up.

'Here you go, Mum,' I say as I hand my mother the cup of tea I have just made her, and I take a few sips of mine before remembering that there is a basket full of washed clothes on my bed that need folding and putting away in the cupboards. I excuse myself to go and do that, leaving a very happy Tuppence with her granny for a little longer, and enter my bedroom to complete another household chore. I fold the clothes and put most of them away where they should be stored, but as I get to my last t-shirt, I accidentally drop it on the floor and when I bend down to pick it up, I notice something poking out from underneath the bed.

I pull it out and realise it's Cameron's book, the one about the missing child, and the one I never finished reading because I was too busy trying to get my own missing child back. Sitting down on the edge of the bed, I open the book and find roughly where I was up to last time before I read a few more chapters again. I tell myself I'm making the most of having my mother here to help with Tuppence and I deserve this brief respite before she goes home and I'm left to carry on being a single mum again. But it's also because I'm curious as to how Cameron ended his fictional story. Surely it ends up differently to how my story ended, right?

I read on, turning the pages as a tale of detectives, journalists and a desperate mother looking for answers is woven, and it all sounds depressingly familiar because I've been through it all in real life. But then, as I'm nearing the end, Cameron delivers what he surely meant to be his shocking twist.

He writes that the father was secretly behind the plot all along.

I stare at the words on the page and try to figure out a way in which this could be a massive coincidence. Cameron couldn't have known that Leon had been behind Tuppence's disappearance, could he? He must have just come up with this ending to the story himself, in his own imagination, and was probably as stunned as I was when it turned out to be the same in real life.

Right?

I lower the book and think about the author in Stirling who wrote this story, sold lots of copies of it and got very rich.

I think about how he was my friend but how I discovered he was keeping things from me too.

Then, I think about how I should probably go and see him one more time.

That's because this story might not quite be over yet.

40

I take the train to Stirling with Mum and Tuppence on a chilly late winter's day, the three of us sitting at a table in a carriage similar to the one I came in with Leon back when life was very different. I can tell Mum still thinks me coming back here is a bad idea because she has had her lips pursed together for most of this trip, a clear sign that she is pensive and unsure. She looks just like she used to when I was younger and told her about a boy I was dating or about some crazy career choice I had decided to pursue on a whim. But I've assured her this trip is necessary for me. This is really it – closure. After today, I know beyond any doubt that I will never set foot in this city again, nor will I need to because I will have done everything I'll ever need to do here by the time the sun sets behind that castle.

As the train reaches Stirling Station, I take Tuppence while Mum brings the bag we brought for her, and we head into the city centre, all three of us wrapped up from the cold weather with coats, hats and gloves. My little girl is in her pram, looking around at everyone and smiling at a few people, far more alert and observant than she was the first time I brought her here. As I promised Mum on the train, we get lunch first, finding a nice Italian restaurant and gorging ourselves on pizza and garlic bread, whilst Tuppence has some mushed up vegetables and flits between enjoying it and screwing her face up at it. Then, once food is out of the way and Mum is in a slightly better mood, I ask her if she can look after Tuppence for me while I go and run a few errands.

'What are you going to do?' Mum wants to know, one eyebrow raised sceptically.

'Don't worry, I'll be back soon,' I say with a smile, keeping things positive and showing her that she has nothing to worry about. Then I walk away, leaving behind the hordes of shoppers and moving onto quieter streets before I eventually come to the quietest street of them all.

I stop and stare at the sign for Buckingham Place and think about how I have gone from hating this place to having more mixed feelings about it now. With Tuppence returned to me, it doesn't hold quite the same power it once did in my mind, and despite that restraining order presumably still being in existence somewhere, I walk past some of the houses here until I reach the door I want.

Knocking, I wait for Raquel to answer, hoping she is in, and when she sees who her visitor is, she looks surprised. But not angry, not like she is going to call the police, and that's good because it gives me the chance to say what I came here to say.

'I'm sorry,' I begin with. 'For accusing you. For breaking into your home. For causing you and your husband stress. I'm really sorry.'

Raquel studies me for a moment before smiling slightly, much to my relief.

'I'm glad you found your daughter,' she says simply. 'Have a wonderful life with her.'

'Enjoy your time with your daughter too,' I say as I see her partner appear in the hallway, holding their girl. When he sees me, he looks worried for a moment, but I just smile at him before wishing Raquel all the best and walking away. But I don't have to go far to see the next person I want to visit while I'm here, only three houses down, in fact, and as I walk up the driveway and pass the expensive car, I admire the stunning home in front of me. This is one of the biggest houses on Buckingham Place and the most recent one to have been sold, eclipsing Cara's home and the price it was purchased for. Apparently, according to the news reports, this home wasn't even on the market, but the prospective buyer made the owners a very generous offer, one they obviously found hard to refuse because they eventually accepted it.

Why was this house sale deemed newsworthy?

Because of the famous buyer.

As the front door opens, I get a look at the new and improved Cameron Cargill. Life has certainly been good to him, and I know that not just by looking at the house he lives in and the car he drives, but his overall appearance. He is slimmer, toned, tanned, healthy. It's easy to exercise, vacation and live a stress-free life when you're stinking rich, and Cameron is certainly that now after his book *The Missing Child* has not only reached the top of the book charts in twelve different countries, but has stayed there for several months.

'Gabby! Hi, what are you doing here? How did you find me?'

'You're a celebrity now,' I say with a smile. 'Did you forget the details of your new mansion were written about by several journalists online?'

'Ahh, that,' Cameron says, scratching his head. 'Yeah, I still need to look at legal action because they shouldn't have shared my address in public, but I've got so much else on my plate right now.'

'I bet! You're an international bestseller. Well done you!'

I smile widely at Cameron to show how proud I am of him. But he still seems a little unsure, probably because the last time he saw me, I was angry at him and stormed away.

'What's going on?' he wants to know.

'Nothing. Everything is great. I was just in the area and thought I'd come and say hi.'

Cameron seems surprised but happy enough that I decided to do that.

'I was so pleased to hear that you got your daughter back,' he says with a smile. 'It was wonderful news.'

'Thank you. Yeah, crazy story, but she's okay and that's all that matters.'

'That's true,' Cameron says before he looks around. 'So, where is she?'

'Tuppence is here in the city with my mum. I'm running a few errands.'

'Errands?'

'Well, not so much errands as apologies.'

'Apologies?'

I look past Cameron and see his expansive hallway and decadent staircase, and he gets the hint.

'Sorry. Please, come in,' he offers.

He steps back and I follow him inside, and he closes the door behind me.

'Can I get you a drink? Tea? Coffee?'

I'm okay, thank you. I can't stay long,' I say as I keep my coat, scarf and gloves on, ready to step back out into the cold in a few moments. 'As I said, I'm here to make a few apologies, and you're one of the people I would like to apologise to.'

'There's no need to-'

'No, there is. I stormed into your book signing and made a scene. I ruined what should have been a special night for you with my crazy ideas and theories. You're not the only one who suffered back then, with me running around this city accusing people of all sorts of things.'

'I understand why you did it,' Cameron says, showing compassion. 'I think anybody would. You were just trying to find your daughter.'

'I know, but regardless of that, I just want to say sorry for any distress I must have caused you. And thank you for your help back then. Without it, I might have given up sooner, and then I never would have found Tuppence.'

Cameron eventually accepts my apology and as he does, I notice a suitcase at the bottom of the stairs.

'You still moving in or taking a trip?' I ask him.

'Taking a trip. I'm off to America for a couple of book events and possibly an appearance on a breakfast show over there.'

'Wow, look at you, Mr Bigshot. How exciting!'

Cameron looks a little embarrassed, and I guess he is still getting used to this new-found fame of his, but I presume he'll only get even more famous if he is headed to meet his readers across The Atlantic.

'There's rumours they might be making my book into a film,' he adds, possibly because he can't resist, and that's even more exciting news.

'Amazing! It just gets better and better,' I say, shaking my head in disbelief. 'Congratulations.'

'Thank you.'

There's a brief silence then and it could easily be the perfect time for me to leave, but before I go, I have a question to ask that has been bugging me for a while.

'I know it was a coincidence that you wrote your story, and it ended up being very similar to what happened in real life with Tuppence and the father being guilty,' I say. 'But I'm curious. Did the police ever come and speak to you to see if it was more than just coincidence?'

'The police?'

'Yeah, I mean, I know you were just writing fiction, but I wondered if the police thought otherwise?'

'A detective did come and speak to me, actually,' Cameron admits. 'Detective Jacobs, I think his name was. He just asked a few questions about where I got my ideas from for the book.'

'And what did you say?'

'I told him the truth. As a crime writer, I draw on inspiration from real-life crime events but then, after that, I simply use my imagination to weave a fictious, entertaining tale. I use a lot of artistic licence, of course.'

'What did he say to that?'

'There wasn't much he could say. He just left.'

I think about that for a moment before shrugging.

'Detective Jacobs is a good man. He would have just been doing his job and double-checking,' I say so that Cameron doesn't worry about it, and he seems fine now.

'Right, I guess I better be going and leave you to pack for America,' I say with a smile. 'Have a great trip.'

'Thanks,' Cameron says as we both make our way to the front door but just before we get there, I stop and reach into my handbag.

'Oh, I almost forgot. Could you sign this for me? It might be worth something one day,' I say with a laugh as I reach into my handbag, and pull out a copy of *The Missing Child.*

'Of course,' Cameron says with a grin as he takes the book. 'I'll just go find a pen.'

I wait in the hallway for Cameron to sign and return the book to me and when he does, I open the first page to see what he has written.

To Gabby, a good friend but an even better mother. All the best, Cameron

'That's lovely, thank you,' I say before putting the book back into my handbag and as Cameron opens the door, he wishes me well again. But while I step outside, I do have one more thing to say to him so I get it off my chest before he can close the door, pack his bags and disappear off to America.

'You saw him, didn't you?' I say calmly.

'Sorry, what?'

'Leon. You saw him that night, taking my baby. You knew exactly what happened, and that's why you were able to write a story that was so close to what turned out to be the truth. The house sale and the father being behind it all. The twists in your book match the real-life story, yet you wrote your book before the truth came out. It's because you knew the truth all along. Isn't that right?'

Cameron looks stunned, but he isn't calling me ridiculous or denying any of it.

'I bet it's why you befriended me,' I go on. 'You wanted to keep an eye on me. See what I knew or was on the verge of finding out. You didn't want the truth coming out too soon, if at all, because you wanted to write your book, and you knew the story was such a good one that it would be rocket fuel for your career.'

Cameron still hasn't spoken, and his silence is very telling. He looks less stunned now and more afraid because I've caught him totally off guard and he isn't able to deny it because he's so surprised.

'I'm right, aren't I?' I ask. 'Just do me the decency of being honest and admit it.'

Cameron says nothing for another moment before finally speaking.

'What are you going to do?' he asks nervously.

I guess that's as close as him admitting to it as I'm going to get.

'Nothing,' I reply simply. 'I just wanted you to know that I know. Goodbye, Cameron.'

I walk away then, leaving behind the lying author, his big house and all the other big houses on this street. I march right past the spot where Tuppence was taken from me and as I leave Buckingham Place, I know I will never be back here again.

But that doesn't mean I won't be hearing about this street one more time.

EPILOGUE

I stop pushing Tuppence's pram when I reach the section of the supermarket where the newspapers are on display. Reaching down, I pick up the nearest tabloid paper and inspect the headline emblazoned across the front page of it. But I could have picked up any newspaper here because they're all leading with the same story.

CRIME AUTHOR DISCOVERED DEAD – POSSIBLE POISONING

Turning the page, I begin reading the article because it's important I keep myself abreast of the story and any developments in terms of the investigation into it.

"Stirling scribe, Cameron Cargill, the author of the bestselling book, The Missing Child, was found dead at his home in the Scottish city four days ago. Today, the police have revealed the cause of death and it's something straight out of the pages of the author's books themselves. Cameron was poisoned, though the police, as of yet, do not know how. The working theory is that he came into contact with something that contained the poison but, so far, there are no suspects and no clue as to how they were able to do this. However, the police are continuing to reassure the general public that there is no risk to them, although until an arrest is made, the residents of Stirling will continue to be on edge."

I put down the newspaper, having got myself up to date with current events, and carry on with my shopping, Tuppence giggling away as we wander the many aisles of this busy supermarket. I see a few people with newspapers in their baskets or trolleys, shoppers who are obviously as eager to catch up on the gripping murder case coming out of Stirling. It's not often Scotland has such a story like this one, a celebrity found dead under suspicious circumstances and on the same street where a child once went missing. I bet it's all the talk in the offices, shops and homes of every city and town across this country. But unlike all these people, I don't need to speculate or guess about what happened to Cameron Cargill.

That's because I already know.

Not long after leaving his home in Stirling after I visited him, I went and found a quiet part of a park, and with nobody around to see me, I used a lighter to set fire to several small items, including my gloves, my handbag and, most importantly of all, the book I had just got Cameron to sign. I burned them all because they were contaminated with a poison I had made myself with items bought in a regular supermarket and using instructions on the internet. I didn't want anybody other than the man I had targeted to come into contact with them and be harmed. Once I had disposed of the evidence, I walked away to go and find Tuppence and my mum and then we went home, back to Edinburgh, leaving Stirling well before the shocking news story was to break.

Cameron never did catch his flight to America, his body discovered by his assistant who had gone to check on him at his house the next day after the author had failed to turn up at the airport or answer his phone.

Of course, he hadn't done any of those things because he had been incapacitated. He would have collapsed about ten minutes after I had asked him to sign the book, his bare hands coming into contact with the poisoned pages and leaving him with no chance of survival.

If only he hadn't signed that book.

Then again, when has an author ever refused to do that?

I killed Cameron because I know he didn't write his book based off of his imagination. He wrote it based off of what he saw and knew. He could have helped me get Tuppence back much sooner than I did, but he decided to keep that information to himself and instead, profit from it by spinning it into a 'fictional' story.

He got what he deserved.

The crime writer has become the crime story himself.

I hope to get away with what I did. I have a feeling I will. Why would anybody suspect me? The rumours online are that Cameron had an obsessed fan, a reader who had read all his books and then crazily decided to poison him just like he had poisoned one of his characters in an earlier book he wrote. That's obviously false, although reading Cameron's earlier work while I was staying at his house was where I got the idea from myself. His book's plot point about poisoning a former lover gave me an idea, and it also made me wonder if he might have poisoned his wife in real life, though he must have covered it up very well if he did.

He should have been more careful with his plot devices. Sharing with his readers in great detail how to do such a thing was risky, though he could never have imagined anybody would be capable of pulling it off in real life.

I could have let Cameron go, but why should I have?

The funny thing is, his book is selling even more copies now he's gone, but I don't care about that.

I got my daughter back.

My story had a happy ending, and that's far better than any work of fiction.

THE END

Thank you for reading

If you would like to receive a FREE copy of my psychological thriller 'Just One Second', then you can find the link to the book at my website www.danielhurstbooks.com

Thank you for reading *The Wife's Baby*. I really hope you enjoyed the story as well as the setting of Stirling, which has become a favourite place of mine to visit ever since I first ventured north to Scotland!

If you have enjoyed this psychological thriller, then you'll be pleased to know that I have several more stories in this genre, and you can find a list of my titles on the next page. These include ***The Doctor's Wife***, which became the #1 selling book in the UK Kindle Store in February 2023, and has now become a four-book series, continuing with ***The Doctor's Widow, The Doctor's Mistress*** and ***The Doctor's Child***.

Other popular titles include ***The Couple's Revenge,*** about two parents trying to save their child from a threat at school, and ***My Daughter's Boyfriend,*** about a mother who follows her daughter to

America to meet her new boyfriend, only to discover a terrible danger awaiting them both…

ALSO BY DANIEL HURST

THE DOCTOR'S WIFE
THE DOCTOR'S WIDOW
THE DOCTOR'S MISTRESS
THE DOCTOR'S CHILD
MY DAUGHTER'S BOYFRIEND
MY DAUGHTER'S HUSBAND
THE COUPLE'S REVENGE
TIL DEATH DO US PART
THE COLLEAGUES
THE PASSENGER
WE USED TO LIVE HERE
THE COUPLE AT TABLE SIX
THE INTRUDER
WHAT MY FAMILY SAW
THE HOLIDAY HOME
HER HUSBAND'S MISTAKE
THE BRIDE TO BE
HER LAST HOUR
THE PERFECT ESCAPE
RUN AWAY WITH ME
THE RIVALS
WE TELL NO ONE
THE WOMAN AT THE DOOR
HE WAS A LIAR
THE BROKEN VOWS
THE WRONG WOMAN
NO TIME TO BE ALONE
THE TUTOR

THE NEIGHBOURS
THE BREAK
THE ROLE MODEL
THE BOYFRIEND
THE PROMOTION
THE NEW FRIENDS
THE ACCIDENT

(All books available now on Amazon and Kindle Unlimited – read on to learn a little more about selected titles...)

THE DOCTOR'S WIFE

The UK Kindle Store #1 Bestseller!

He thinks his secret is safe. But she knows the truth…

My husband is a doctor. He's smart and charming and everybody trusts him. **Except me.**

On the surface, it looks like I have it all – the perfect marriage, the perfect husband, the perfect life. But it's far from the truth. **Doctor Drew Devlin** is not the respectable figure he makes out to be. The reason we moved to this beautiful, old property with a gorgeous view of the sea was because we needed to put our past behind us. It should've been a fresh start for us both.

Except I've discovered my husband has been lying to me again. He's using the power he has in his job to mess with people's lives, and to get exactly what he wants – no matter who it hurts. But he's underestimated me. I've had plenty of time, in this big, isolated house, to think about all of his mistakes. *And my husband has no idea what's about to happen next…*

If you enjoy this, the series continues with The Doctor's Widow!

THE COUPLE'S REVENGE

How far would you go to protect your child?

I knew something was wrong. It's a mother's instinct. I could tell when my son started hiding things from me. He used to walk to school with a mischievous grin on his beautiful face. Now he avoids eye contact and keeps his head down.

Since I discovered he's being bullied by a classmate, I've spent every day worrying, my stomach churning with anxiety from the moment he leaves the house to the second he walks back through the door. Everyone keeps telling me I'm overreacting, but I won't risk my child's safety. My husband and I try to talk to the other boy's parents, but it only makes things worse…

Then our precious child is hurt. Enough is enough. It has to stop. Even if that means taking matters into our own hands. Because we know the truth about the family targeting our son – it's not the first time they've done this.

So the question is, exactly how far will we go to get revenge?

TIL DEATH DO US PART

What if your husband was your worst enemy?

Megan thinks that she has the perfect husband and the perfect life. Craig works all day so that she doesn't have to, leaving her free to relax in their beautiful and secluded country home. But when she starts to long for friends and purpose again, Megan applies for a job in London, much to her husband's disappointment. She thinks he is upset because she is unhappy. But she has no idea.

When Megan secretly attends an interview and meets a recruiter for a drink, Craig decides it is time to act. Locking her away in their home, Megan realises that her husband never had her best interests at heart. Worse, they didn't meet by accident. Craig has been planning it all from the start.

As Megan is kept shut away from the world with only somebody else's diary for company, she starts to uncover the lies, the secrets, and the fact that she isn't actually Craig's first wife after all...

THE PASSENGER

She takes the same train every day. But this is a journey she will never forget…

Amanda is a hard-working single mum, focused on her job and her daughter, Louise. But it's also time she did something for herself, and after saving for years, she is now close to quitting her dreary 9-5 and following her dream.

But then, on her usual commute home from London to Brighton, she meets a charming stranger – a man who seems to know everything about her. Then he delivers an ultimatum. She needs to give him the code to her safe where she keeps her savings before they reach Brighton – or she will never see Louise again.

Amanda is horrified, but while she knows the threat is real, she can't give him the code. That's because the safe contains something other than her money. It holds a secret. *A secret so terrible it will destroy both her's and her daughter's life if it ever gets out…*

THE NEIGHBOURS

It seemed like the perfect house on the perfect street. *Until they met the neighbours...*

Happily married couple, Katie and Sean, have plenty to look forward to as they move into their new home and plan for the future. But then they meet two of their new neighbours, and everything on their quiet street suddenly doesn't seem as desirable as it did before.

Having been warned about the other neighbours and their adulterous and criminal ways, Katie and Sean realise that they are going to have to be on their guard if they want to make their time here a happy one.

But some of the other neighbours seem so nice, and that's why they choose to ignore the warning and get friendly with the rest of the people on the street. *And that is why their marriage will never be the same again...*

THE TUTOR

What if you invited danger into your home?

Amy is a loving wife and mother to her husband, Nick, and her two children, Michael and Bella. It's that dedication to her family that causes her to seek help for her teenage son when it becomes apparent that he is going to fail his end of school exams.

Enlisting the help of a professional tutor, Amy is certain that she is doing the best thing for her son and, indeed, her family. But when she discovers that there is more to this tutor than meets the eye, it is already too late.

With the rest of her family enamoured by the tutor, Amy is the only one who can see that there is something not quite right about her. But as the tutor becomes more involved in Amy's family, it's not just the present that is threatened. Secrets from the past are exposed too, and by the time everything is out in the open, Amy isn't just worried about her son and his exams anymore. She is worried for the survival of her entire family.

HE WAS A LIAR

What if you never really knew the man you loved?

Sarah is in a loving relationship with Paul, a seemingly perfect man who she is hoping to marry and start a family with one day, until his sudden death sends her into a world of pain.

Trying to come to terms with her loss, Sarah finds comfort in going through some of Paul's old things, including his laptop and his emails. But after finding something troubling, Sarah begins to learn things about Paul that she never knew before, and it turns out he wasn't as perfect as she thought. But as she unravels more about his secretive past, she ends up not only learning things that break her heart, but things that the police will be interested to know too.

Sarah can't believe what she has discovered. But it's only when she keeps digging that she realises it's not just her late boyfriend's secrets that are contained on the laptop. Other people's secrets are too, and they aren't dead, which means they will do anything to protect them.

RUN AWAY WITH ME

What if your partner was wanted by the police?

Laura is feeling content with her life. She is married, she has a good home, and she is due to give birth to her first child any day now. But her perfect world is shattered when her husband comes home flustered and afraid. He's made a terrible mistake. He's done a bad thing. *And now the police are going to be looking for him.*

There's only one way out of this. He wants to run. *But he won't go without his wife…*

Laura knows it is wrong. She knows they should stay and face the music. But she doesn't want to lose her man. She can't raise this baby alone. *So she agrees to go with him.* But life on the run is stressful and unpredictable, and as time goes by, Laura worries she has made a terrible mistake. They should never have ran. But it's too late for that now. Her life is ruined. The only question is: *how will it end?*

THE ROLE MODEL

She raised her. Now she must help her…

Heather is a single mum who has always done what's best for her daughter, Chloe. From childhood up to the age of seventeen, Chloe has been no trouble. That is until one night when she calls her mother with some shocking news. There's been an accident. *And now there's a dead body…*

As always, Heather puts her daughter's safety before all else, but this might be one time when she goes too far. Instead of calling the emergency services, Heather hides the body, saving her daughter from police interviews and public outcry.

But as she well knows, everything she does has an impact on her child's behaviour, and as time goes on and the pair struggle to keep their sordid secret hidden, Heather begins to think that she hasn't been such a good mum after all. *In fact, she might have been the worst role model ever…*

THE BROKEN VOWS

He broke his word to her. Now she wants revenge…

Alison is happily married to Graham, or at least she is until she finds out that he has been cheating on her. Graham has broken the vows he made on his wedding day. How could he do it? It takes Alison a while to figure it out, but at least she has time on her side. *Only that is where she is wrong.*

A devastating diagnosis means the clock is ticking down on her life now, and if she wants revenge on her cheating partner, then she is going to have to act fast. Alison does just that, implementing a dangerous and deadly plan, and it's one that will have far reaching consequences for several people, including her clueless husband.

WE USED TO LIVE HERE

How much do you know about your house?

When the Burgess family move into their 'forever' home, it seems like they are set for many happy years together at their new address. Steph and Grant, along with their two children, Charlie and Amelia, settle into their new surroundings quickly. But then they receive a visit from a couple who claim to have lived in their house before and wish to have a look around for old times' sake. They seem pleasant and plausible, so Steph invites them in. And that's when things start to change…

It's not long after the peculiar visit when the homeowners start to find evidence of the past all around their new home as they redecorate. But it's the discovery of a hidden wall containing several troubling messages that really sends Steph into a spin, and after digging deeper into the history of the house a little more, she learns it is connected to a shocking crime from the past. *A crime that still remains unsolved...*

Every house has secrets. But some don't stay buried forever…

THE 20 MINUTES SERIES

What readers are saying:

"If you like people-watching, then you will love these books!"

"The psychological insight was fascinating, the stories were absorbing and the characters were 3D. I absolutely loved it."

"The books in this series are an incredibly easy read, you become invested in the lives of the characters so easily, and I am eager to know more and more. Roll on the next book."

THE 20 MINUTES SERIES (in order)

20 MINUTES ON THE TUBE
20 MINUTES LATER
20 MINUTES IN THE PARK
20 MINUTES ON HOLIDAY
20 MINUTES BY THE THAMES
20 MINUTES AT HALLOWEEN
20 MINUTES AROUND THE BONFIRE
20 MINUTES BEFORE CHRISTMAS
20 MINUTES OF VALENTINE'S DAY
20 MINUTES TO CHANGE A LIFE
20 MINUTES IN LAS VEGAS
20 MINUTES IN THE DESERT

20 MINUTES ON THE ROAD
20 MINUTES BEFORE THE WEDDING
20 MINUTES IN COURT
20 MINUTES BEHIND BARS
20 MINUTES TO MIDNIGHT
20 MINUTES BEFORE TAKE OFF
20 MINUTES IN THE AIR
20 MINUTES UNTIL IT'S OVER

About The Author

Daniel Hurst lives in the Northwest of England with his wife, Harriet, and daughter, Penny, and if that doesn't make him lucky enough, he considers himself extremely fortunate to be able to write stories every day for his readers.

You can visit him at his online home www.danielhurstbooks.com

You can connect with Daniel on Facebook at www.facebook.com/danielhurstbooks or on Instagram at www.instagram.com/danielhurstbooks

He is always happy to receive emails from readers at daniel@danielhurstbooks.com and replies to every single one.

Thank you for reading.

Daniel

THE WIFE'S BABY by Daniel Hurst published by Daniel Hurst Books Limited, The Coach House, 31 View Road, Rainhill, Merseyside, L35 0LF

Front Cover Design by 100Covers

Made in the USA
Middletown, DE
04 May 2024

53854861R00181